Eventually he said, "So what would you do to keep the resort open?"

Panic kicked her in the stomach. "I—what? What could I do?"

He walked across the veranda, stopping so close she could see the white flash of his narrow smile. "Keeping Sea Winds going would be a sacrifice for me—I'm asking what you're prepared to sacrifice for your friends."

Blood pumped through her, awakening her body to urgent life, but her brain seemed to have been overwhelmed by lethargy. She moistened her lips and croaked, "If you mean what I think you're meaning..."

"That's exactly what I mean," he said, that note of ironic amusement more pronounced. "I want you, Alli. You must have guessed—it's not as though you're a sweet little innocent."

Stunned, she licked her lips and swallowed. "You're going to have to be clearer than that."

Boredom descended like a mask over his face. "Really?" he mocked, his mouth twisting. "Then perhaps I should demonstrate."

And he kissed her.

ROBYN DONALD has always lived in Northland in New Zealand, initially on her father's stud dairy farm in Warkworth, then in the Bay of Islands, an area of great natural beauty, where she lives today with her husband and an ebullient and mostly Labrador dog. She resigned her teaching position when she found she enjoyed writing romance fiction more, and now spends any time not writing in reading, gardening, traveling and writing letters to keep up with her two adult children and her friends.

RUTHLESS BILLIONAIRE, INEXPERIENCED MISTRESS

ROBYN DONALD

~ HIS VIRGIN MISTRESS ~

HARLEQUIN®

TORONTO • NEW YORK • LONDON
AMSTERDAM • PARIS • SYDNEY • HAMBURG
STOCKHOLM • ATHENS • TOKYO • MILAN • MADRID
PRAGUE • WARSAW • BUDAPEST • AUCKLAND

Recycling programs
for this product may
not exist in your area.

ISBN-13: 978-0-373-52702-1
ISBN-10:   0-373-52702-0

RUTHLESS BILLIONAIRE, INEXPERIENCED MISTRESS

First North American Publication 2007.
This edition 2009.

Previously published in the U.K. under the title
THE BILLIONAIRE'S PASSION.

Copyright © 2004 by Robyn Donald.

RUTHLESS BILLIONAIRE, INEXPERIENCED MISTRESS

ROBYN DONALD

CHAPTER ONE

ALLI PIERCE wove another frangipani blossom into the lei. After an appreciative sniff of the perfume from its shameless golden throat, she said, 'I'm completely determined to get to New Zealand, but I won't sell myself for the fare!'

'I know that,' her friend Sisilu said peaceably in the local variation of the language the Polynesians had carried across the immense reaches of the Pacific Ocean. 'Calm down. It was just a comment Fili made.'

'What's the matter with her lately? She's turned into a nasty little witch.'

Sisilu grinned. 'You're so naïve! She's mad with you because she's got a serious crush on Tama, but he's got a serious crush on you. And she still reckons it's unfair that just because you've got a New Zealand passport Barry pays you New Zealand wages and not island ones. After all, you've been living on Valanu since you were a couple of months old.'

Alli anchored a lock of damp red-brown hair away from her hot face with a carved shell comb. 'Actually, I agree with her,' she said honestly. 'It makes me feel guilty, but Barry says it's company policy.'

'He'd know. Have you seen the new owner yet?'

'New owner?' She stared at her friend. 'Sea Winds's new owner? Here?'

Sisilu's dark eyes gleamed with sly amusement. 'Right here in throbbing, downtown Valanu.'

Alli laughed. 'Big deal.' But she sobered immediately. 'No, I haven't seen him—you know Monday's my day off. When did he get here?'

'Last night—arrived out of the blue on a private plane.'

A frown drew Alli's winged brows together. 'I thought Sea Winds was sold to a huge worldwide organisation. The head guy wouldn't come here—too busy being a tycoon. This man is probably just some suit from management. What's he like?'

'Big,' Sisilu told her, with a sensuous intonation that told Alli the new owner was tall, not fat. She sighed with purely feminine appreciation. 'And he's got presence—he's the owner all right. Not that I've seen much of him. He's been shut up with Barry all day, but he did a quick tour of the resort while we were rehearsing this morning.'

Alli's frown deepened. 'If he's the owner,' she said forthrightly, deft hands weaving more flowers into the lei, 'I'll bet that as well as being tall he's middle-aged, paunchy and going bald.'

Sisilu rolled bold dark eyes. 'I should take you up on that—it would be easy money! You couldn't be more wrong. He's got wide shoulders and long, strong legs—not a clumsy bone in his body and a stomach as flat as mine or yours. Flatter, probably.' Sisilu counted off his assets with frank relish. 'Slade Hawkings walks like a chief, looks like a chief, talks like a chief—he's already got the girls buzzing.'

Hawkings? Surprise scuttled on chilly feet down

Alli's spine, but it was a common enough name in the English-speaking world.

Don't go imagining bogeymen, she warned herself. 'If he is the owner—or even an executive with power—he won't be interested in us islanders.' And to banish the cold needle of alarm she added briskly, 'So the girls might as well stop buzzing. Apart from the fact that he probably lives in America or England or Switzerland, men like him go for women who are sophisticated and knowledgeable.'

'If he's a day over twenty-eight I'll eat this lei,' Sisilu said cheerfully. Her tone altered when she said with a sideways look, 'As for that crack about middle-aged men—it just shows what a baby you are; the middle-aged ones are the ones to watch. Which is why you should be keeping an eye on Barry.'

'Barry?' Alli stared at her in astonishment. When her companion nodded, she went on with heavy sarcasm, 'You mean Barry Simcox? The hotel manager who was utterly broken-hearted when his wife ran back to Australia with their little boy because she couldn't stand living in this "godforsaken island in the middle of the Pacific Ocean"? I quote, of course. *That* Barry—who has never even looked sideways at me?'

'*That* very same Barry,' Sisilu said with a toss of her head. 'You might not have seen him looking at you, but others have.'

Alli snorted.

'Well, don't say I didn't warn you.' Her friend went on. 'The new owner would be a much better lover. He looks like a film star, only tougher.' After an elaborate sigh she added, 'And you can tell by

looking at him that he knows what he's doing when
it comes to making love—he's got that aura, you
know?'

'Well, no, I don't know.'

Sisilu eyed a hibiscus flower with a critical frown
before discarding it. It fell with a soft plop onto the
floor. 'Oh, yes, you do.' She added slyly, 'Tama has
it too.'

Tama was the second son of the island chief, and
Sisilu's cousin. Alli flushed. 'I wish he hadn't decided
he is in love with me.'

'It's because you're not in love with him,' Sisilu
said wisely, choosing another bloom. 'And because
you're different—you don't want him when every
other girl in Valanu would happily take him for a
lover. As well, of course, virgins are special in our
culture. Don't worry about him; he'll get over it once
you leave.'

Both worked in silence for a few minutes before
Sisilu ruthlessly dragged the conversation back to the
topic foremost in her mind. 'And the new owner does
not live in Switzerland or England or America—he
lives in New Zealand.'

'So do about four million other people.'

'As for the sort of women he likes—when he saw
you walk across the foyer five minutes ago he looked
as though he'd been hit in the face with a dead shark.
I know *that* look too,' Sisilu finished smugly.

In her driest voice Alli said, 'I'm sure you do—but
are you certain it wasn't you he was watching? After
all, you're the most beautiful girl in Valanu.'

Sisilu said prosaically, 'He didn't even see me.'

'Wait 'til he does.' Busy fingers pausing, Alli

watched her friend thread several more hibiscus flowers into a head lei. Dark as blood, rich as passion, they glowed with silken light. 'Anyway, if he's that gorgeous he's probably gay.'

Sisilu's laugh demolished that idea. 'Far from it. When he looked at you he liked what he saw. He might be interested in helping a countrywoman, especially if you gave him an incentive.'

'Not that sort of incentive, thank you very much,' Alli returned with robust forthrightness, threading in several long pointed leaves to give the effect of a ruff. 'If he wants to help me he can keep the resort going.'

It was the only chance she had to save enough for her fare to New Zealand.

Her friend ignored her. 'Making love with him would not be difficult. He has the kind of sexuality that sets off fires. I wish he'd forget he's the boss and look my way.'

Alli closed her eyes against the shimmer of the sun on the lagoon. Beneath the high-pitched shriek of a gull she could hear the slow, deep roar of the Pacific combers smashing onto the coral reef.

The girls she'd grown up with on Valanu had a forthright, honest appreciation of their sexuality. Once married they'd stay faithful, but until then they enjoyed the pleasures of the flesh without shame.

Alli's father had seen to it that she didn't follow suit.

'Why are you so keen to leave Valanu?' Sisilu asked unexpectedly. 'It's your home.'

Alli shrugged, slender golden fingers still for a second before she picked up another flower from the fragrant heap beside her. Her generous mouth hardened. 'I want to know why my mother left us, and what drove my father to hide himself away here.'

'You know why. He went to school with the chief in Auckland. Naturally, when the tribal corporation wanted someone to run the system, they thought of him.'

Golden-brown eyes sombre, Alli nodded. 'But there are too many questions. Dad wouldn't say a word about any family. I don't even know who my grandparents were.'

Her friend made a clucking noise. To be deprived of family in Polynesia meant much the same as being an outcast. 'Your father was a good man,' she said quickly.

Two years previously, after Ian Pierce's death, Alli had gone through his papers and found the one thing she'd longed to know—the name of her mother. That find had encouraged her to save the money she needed to pay an investigator to find Marian Hawkings. Three months previously the dossier had arrived. Now she was saving desperately to meet the woman who'd borne her, only to abandon her.

She said steadily, 'My mother was an Englishwoman who married Dad in England and came to New Zealand with him. After they divorced she married another man, but she's a widow now, still living in Auckland. I don't want to intrude into her life—I just want to know a few things. Then I'll have some sort of closure.' She concentrated on weaving the final flower into the lei.

Her friend's shoulders lifted. 'But you'll come back, won't you? We are your family now.'

Alli smiled mistily, deft fingers flying as they tied

off the lei with long strings of *tii* leaf. 'And I couldn't have a kinder one. It's just that the need to know gnaws at my heart.'

'I understand.' Sisilu grinned. 'Anyway, you'll hate New Zealand. It's big and cold and different—no place for someone who loves Valanu as much as you.'

She looked up as a woman strode towards them. 'Uh-oh, here's trouble,' she said beneath her breath. 'Look at her face!'

Without preamble the trainer of the dance troupe said, 'Alli, you'll be dancing tonight—Fili's sick. And we need to make a good impression because the owner of the hotel is deciding whether to keep Sea Winds open or close it down.'

Both girls stared at her. 'He can't do that,' Alli blurted.

'Of course he can, and from what I'm hearing he'd do it without thinking twice. When it was first built it paid its way, but the war in Sant'Rosa cut off the supply of tourists, and for the past five years it's been losing more and more each year,' the older woman said bluntly.

Alli frowned. 'If things are that bad, why did the new owner buy it?'

'Who knows?' She picked up one of the lei and examined it, then dropped it and turned away. 'Perhaps he was cheated. Although he doesn't look like a man who'd allow that to happen to him. It isn't any of our business, anyway, but make sure you dance well tonight.'

Aware that she was a widow, whose job at the resort paid for the schooling of her three sons, both girls watched her go.

Soberly Alli said, 'If the resort closes it will be a disaster for Valanu.'

Sisilu said with a wry smile, 'So perhaps if the owner likes what he sees when he looks at you it will help all of us if you are nice to him. You might be able to influence him into keeping the hotel open.'

As she dressed for the dancing that night, Alli remembered the hidden worry in her friend's voice. The man who'd caused this fear hadn't eaten in the restaurant, but he'd be there for the floorshow, watching from somewhere in the darkness of the wide terrace. The women getting ready in the staff cloakroom were more silent than usual; already everyone knew that the resort was threatened.

'He's there, so no giggling,' the organiser said sternly as excited yells and applause from the audience indicated that the men's posture dance had reached its climax. She cast an eye over Alli and her face softened. 'You look good—those cream frangipani suit your skin and your red hair.'

That was about the only thing she'd inherited from her mother. Shortly after her father's death Alli had found his wedding certificate, and with it a photograph—her father, looking so proud of himself she almost hadn't recognised him, and a laughing woman. Apart from hair colour, Alli didn't look at all like her mother, but the wedding certificate attached to the photograph implied that this woman had borne her.

And then left her. With the marriage certificate and the photograph had been a legal notification of divorce, and a newspaper clipping about her mother's marriage a couple of years later to another man.

The staccato rhythm of the drums settled into a

sultry beat, and she and the other dancers took their places in the line. Alli adjusted the uncomfortable bra and began singing an old island love song. The dancers filed out from behind the woven screen that shielded the door from the audience, voices blending in harmony, mobile hands eloquently conveying the story.

From the darkness behind the diners, Slade watched them with a critical eye; amateurs they might be, but they were good. Unfortunately the hokey bras made of half-coconuts detracted from the effect. If he decided to keep the place open they'd go.

Not that the audience cared. His mouth curved in a cynical smile as he surveyed the enthusiastic group of diners.

Give them erotically charged lyrics and lithe bodies polished by the light of flares, dark eyes that beckoned from beneath garlands of perfumed flowers, white teeth flashing in come-hither smiles, and they were more than happy.

He examined the dancers again, realising with sardonic derision that his gaze kept drifting back to Alli Pierce. His chief troubleshooter had come back with photographs of her, but none had done her justice. In them she'd looked young and enthusiastic, whereas in the flesh the overwhelming impression was of glowing, sensuous freshness emphasised by tilted lion-coloured eyes, a laughing provocative mouth, and dramatic cheekbones.

Although she danced with tantalising grace, and managed to look both innocent and seductive festooned with wreaths of flowers and green leaves, her hands fluttering in stylised, exquisite movements, that sensual, enticing surface was a lie.

Beautiful, sexy and twenty years old, it seemed that Alli Pierce had decided on a career as a con artist.

Ignoring an unwelcome itch of desire, he focused on her with the keen brain and ferocious concentration that had propelled his father's thriving local organisation onto the world stage. The investigator he'd dispatched to the island had learned that her father had brought her there as a baby, and that the locals didn't believe she had Polynesian ancestry.

'Not,' the investigator had told him wearily, 'that they were at all forthcoming about her or her father.'

Slade's brows shot up. 'I thought places like Valanu were hotbeds of gossip.'

'But not to outsiders.' The middle-aged woman shrugged. 'They were extremely protective of her. I did manage to find out that the hotel manager's wife left him because of Ms Pierce, but the next person I talked to about it said that that was a lie.'

'What do you think?'

The older woman's expression turned cynical. 'The people there have a pretty liberated attitude to premarital sex, and she certainly seems like the other girls—flirtatious and light-hearted. I saw her several times with the manager and he's certainly hot for her. But so is one of the local boys—the chief's second son. She could be running them both, of course.'

Indeed she could, Slade thought as he watched the way the torches summoned mahogany flames from her long, flower-studded hair. Only slightly taller than the other women, she was built on more racy lines, and her skin gleamed gold rather than bronze.

And he shouldn't be eyeing her like some old lecher in an oriental slave market; he was supposed to be grading the show. Ruthlessly he bent his attention to the other dancers, the ambience, the effect of the whole package on the audience.

Song and dance finished on a sweetly melancholy note; after a moment's silence the audience erupted in exuberant applause, and the dancers, laughing, swung into a fast, upbeat Valanuan version of a hula.

Slade watched hips swinging suggestively, hands sinuously alluring and smiles that tempted every man in the audience—including him, he realised with disgust. Exasperated by the pagan appetite stirring into awareness, he sensed someone's arrival beside him.

'For amateurs, we think they're pretty good,' the manager said, his voice too easy and confident for a man who knew his job was on the line.

'Of their sort, excellent,' Slade said casually. 'Who are they?'

'Oh, just local girls—most of them are staff. The one on the far left teaches at the local school, and second from right is Alli Pierce, whose father was a New Zealander, like you. She's not a regular, but one of the girls is ill tonight so she's taken her place.'

'The girl who works in the souvenir shop?'

And possibly the mistress of the man beside him; there had been a far from fatherly intonation in the manager's voice when he spoke of her, and he certainly paid her three times the local wage. As she conveniently lived in a house next door to Simcox's, the accusation was probably correct.

Eyes fixed on the dancers, the man beside him nodded. 'Ian Pierce brought Alli to Vanalu when she was a baby; apparently her mother died in an accident when she was only a couple of weeks old.' His voice altered fractionally. 'She's a lovely girl, and she deserves more than Valanu can offer her.'

And you'd like to provide it, Slade thought grimly. His narrowed eyes followed Alli Pierce as the line of dancers swayed off into the darkness, his body tightening when she turned just before she stepped out of the light of the flares and looked directly at him.

Transfixed by a feral response to that swift glance, he barely noticed the three men who leapt out with a wild yell above a sudden clamour of drums.

Angrily he summoned the ragged remnants of his self-control; in his relationships he required much more than lust, the lowest common denominator. Hell, it had been years since his hormones had driven him along that bleak path.

Droning like a distant engine, the manager's voice intruded into his thoughts. Slade forced his mind away from an inviting, enticing face.

'Bright too,' the man was saying. 'But her father wouldn't hear of her going to a better high school in New Zealand. It's a shame she's stuck here—she'd do well if she had more opportunity.'

Slade thought cynically that she hoped to force that opportunity by extracting money from a total stranger.

Marian wasn't going to be her ticket to a newer, better life. Shocked and bewildered by the letter Alli Pierce had sent her, his stepmother had done what she did whenever she was faced by something she couldn't handle—turned to Slade.

An image of the girl's face flashed with teasing seductiveness against his eyelids. He'd see her tomorrow and he'd scare the hell out of her—and enjoy doing it. Of all forms of crime, blackmail came close to being the most despicable.

And while he was doing it he'd find out why she'd targeted his stepmother.

In the small room where the dancers were getting out of their uncomfortable bras and the pareus swathed tightly around their hips, Sisilu said gleefully, 'He was staring at you. See, I told you he was interested! And so are you.'

'I am not!'

'Then why did you turn around to stare at him?' her friend demanded unanswerably.

Alli rubbed her palms over her cold upper arms and muttered, 'I just wanted to see what he looked like.'

'You felt him watching you.' Sisilu nodded wisely and quoted a local proverb about eyes being the arrows of love.

'Oh, rubbish,' Alli said, knotting her own pareu above her breasts.

In fact, she didn't know why she'd acted on that compelling impulse, but she could see him now as if he stood in front of her—a tall man, broad-shouldered and formidable, the starkly moulded framework of his face picked out by a spurt of flame from the torches. He exuded authority and a compelling magnetism that still kept her pulse soaring.

'Well, what did you think of him?' Sisilu asked.

'He has presence,' Alli admitted grudgingly, pushing her hair back off her damp cheeks.

Sisilu laughed, but to Alli's relief left the subject alone.

An hour or so later, at home in the small house she'd shared with her father, she recalled the swift, hot contraction in the pit of her stomach when her gaze had clashed with that of the new owner. For a stretched moment the laughter and applause had faded into a thick, tense silence. Although it was sheer fantasy, she felt as though they'd duelled across the hot, crowded space, like old enemies—or old lovers.

'You're just imagining things,' she scoffed. 'You could barely see him.'

On an impulse she went to the safe and took out the folder containing all that she had of her family— the photograph of her father and mother, the legal certificates with their alien names, the newspaper cutting.

Why had her father changed his name when he came to Valanu? And hers too. It made her feel as though she'd been living a lie for twenty years.

Carefully she unfolded the newspaper clipping. Dated three years after her birth, a year after her parents' divorce, it told of the wedding between Marian Carter and David Hawkings.

If there'd been a photograph of the newlyweds she'd have been able to judge whether Slade Hawkings looked anything like David Hawkings.

'No, it's too far-fetched; coincidences like that don't happen,' she reassured herself, and went to bed, where she lay awake for hours before sinking into a restless, dream-disturbed sleep.

Of course in the morning she woke too late to swim in the lagoon. As it was, she'd opened the doors of the shop only seconds before the first influx of customers arrived—a group of young men from America on a diving holiday.

They swarmed around her, teasing, laughing, flirting enthusiastically, but without any sign of seriousness. Because there was no harm in any of them, she laughed, teased and flirted back.

However, there was always one who pushed his luck; smiling, she eluded his hands, turning him off with a quip that made him yell with laughter.

He was saying with an overdone leer, 'Same time tonight, honey?' when Barry Simcox arrived.

Previously she'd have thought nothing of Barry's frown, and the way he watched the young man, but Sisilu's comment the previous day had put an uneasy dent in her easygoing friendship with the manager.

Once the divers left the shop, Barry came in. And with him came the new owner.

Alli's heart jumped so strongly she had to stop herself from pressing her hand over it to keep it in place. In the soft, bewitching clarity of morning Slade Hawkings looked even more forbidding than he had in the dramatic light of the flares.

Fussily, Barry performed the introductions. 'Mr Hawkings is here to check us over,' he said with a smile that just missed its mark. He turned to Slade and informed him, 'As you've seen from the figures, Alli has done well with the souvenir shop.'

Alli held out her hand and said quietly, 'How do you do?'

Green eyes, translucent and emotionless as glass, examined her—almost, she thought, as though she'd surprised him. His hand was warm, but not unpleasantly so, and dry, yet she sensed latent power in the lean fingers and brief grip. He didn't wring her fingers painfully together as many men did.

Colour heated her skin at the memory of Sisilu's summing up—this was definitely a man who knew women.

'How do you do?' Slade Hawkings returned in a deep, cool voice, dismissing her with his tone and the flick of a humourless smile.

Stung, Alli stiffened her spine. OK, so he was the boss, and the powerful angles and planes of his face were both compelling and daunting, but he had no reason to look at her as though she were rubbish underneath his shoes.

She turned to put out more stock, but Slade Hawkings said levelly, 'I'd like you to stay, please.'

So she waited in outwardly respectful silence while the two men discussed the shop at length.

Slade Hawkings commented, 'Stone carving isn't an art that Pacific Islanders are noted for. Why are you selling this stuff here?'

Barry opened his mouth to answer, but in a voice that stopped the other man's words before they could be uttered, Slade said, 'Alli.'

'We used to stock woven bags,' she told him, bristling, 'but the customs officers in New Zealand and Australia thought they might hide insects. Since fumigation doesn't do much for a bag, I looked around for something else.'

Slade nodded. 'And imported this cheap product to take their place?'

In a tone so courteous it skidded dangerously close to insolence, she said, 'They are not imported—there's always been carving on Valanu. Because there were no large trees on the atoll, the islanders worked coral instead. These are god figures—not the most sacred, of course, but they're carved with skill and all the correct ceremonies.' She indicated an eye-catching quilt on the wall. 'These are not imports, either. A woman whose mother was a Cook Islander showed the Valanuans how to make them. They're hugely popular, but I do make sure the buyers know they aren't a traditional craft on Valanu.'

She expected him to blench at the pattern of bold scarlet and white lilies, but he startled her by saying, 'I hope you're paying enough for them—they take years to finish.'

In answer she flicked the tag around so that he could see the price. He leaned over her shoulder to look, and she breathed in a hint of elusive scent.

Undiluted essence of male, she thought wildly—no hint of cologne or soap, just a faint whisper of fragrance, clean and salty and intensely personal. Astonished, she felt her mouth dry and her skin tighten unbearably. His closeness beat against her like a dark force of nature.

Appalled by her reaction, she dropped her hand and clenched it at her side, not daring to move in case she touched him. The only sound she could hear was the uneven thudding of her heart.

Then he stepped back, snapping the invisible bonds that had locked her into a trance.

Alli forced her face to register a bland lack of interest before turning to face him. Eyes as cold as polar ice and every bit as hard met hers.

'Do you sell many?' he asked laconically.

Alli's chin tilted. 'At least one a month. We'd sell more if we could get them. They're popular.'

'You look very young to be managing this shop,' he observed.

Barry jumped in. 'Since Alli's been here she's increased turnover considerably. She speaks the local language as well as English so she's an excellent liaison with the craftspeople on the island. And she has great taste, as you can see.'

Slade Hawkings's eyes turned colder, if that was possible. Ignoring the other man, he asked her about the turnover, about her ordering, relentlessly making her justify everything she'd done.

When he left half an hour later she felt as though he'd wrung every scrap of information from her. Shaking inside, she watched him stride beside the manager across the foyer, tall and lithe—a true chief, wearing his inborn authority with panache.

Or, considering him from another angle, a shark, right at the top of the food chain!

CHAPTER TWO

HER mouth parched from Slade Hawkings's grilling, Alli poured herself a glass of pineapple juice, but had only swallowed a little when the after-breakfast customers arrived.

It turned out to be one of those days—hot, busy, with more than its fair share of irritating and irritated people. When she closed the doors at seven that night she was tired and hungry and badly in need of a swim. At least Fili had recovered enough to dance, so she didn't have to don the outrageously uncomfortable coconut bra!

The new owner of the resort had passed through the foyer a couple of times, cool and utterly sure of himself—the consummate predator. Beside him, Barry's fraying composure marked him as prey.

'Like the rest of us,' Sisilu said forthrightly when Alli hurried in to say hello before the show. 'Everyone's walking around as though they might tread on a stonefish.'

'Surely he wouldn't just close Sea Winds down and walk away from it—apart from anything else, the buildings are worth a lot of money.'

'He's a very rich man—someone said he's a billionaire now.' Sisilu shrugged as though that explained everything. 'You don't get where he is by not making hard decisions. And he's not here to lie on the beach and work on his tan; he came here to do something. It's like he's electrified the whole place.'

'With the sheer force of his personality?' Alli jeered. 'No matter what he was like everyone would be jumpy; people tend to get stressed when their jobs are at stake.'

'But this feels personal,' her friend said abruptly. 'He's got it in for someone. All right, you laugh— but he's a man who makes things happen, and something's going to happen now. I can feel it.'

Strolling towards the lagoon across sand still warm from the day's heat, Alli pondered Sisilu's words. In the distance she could hear the feverish drumming that heralded the fire dancers, and said a silent prayer for them all.

At the water's edge she dropped her pareu into a heap and walked out into the lukewarm water, sinking into it with a long sigh of relief.

Personal? No, how could it be? Sisilu was reacting morbidly to the situation.

But as Alli struck out parallel to the beach she wondered in selfish frustration why Slade Hawkings couldn't have waited another six months to buy the resort. By then she'd have saved enough to pay her passage to New Zealand—first the several days' trip to Fiji on a copra boat, then a flight to Auckland.

Her jaw tightened. She'd find a way to get there; no arrogant hotel owner was going to stop her. She had a mission, and she'd see it through.

Buoyed by the silken water, she floated on her back and stared at the stars, huge and white and aloof, their lovely, liquid Polynesian names more real to her than the ones her father had given them. They'd be different in New Zealand. And she'd be leaving behind her all her friends, a familiar, comfortable way of life…

She fought back a nascent shiver of homesickness. Much as she'd miss the island and her friends, she wanted more than Valanu could offer. And, judging by Slade Hawkings's attitude, even if he didn't close down Sea Winds she had no future there.

Diving as easily as the dolphins that sometimes visited the lagoon, she breathed out slowly and swam through a silvery wonderland towards the beach. Eventually her toes found the sand; frowning, she stood and wiped the water from her eyes, because someone waited for her beside the small pile of her pareu.

Tama.

Oh, not now, Alli thought wearily, and then felt mean. He didn't *want* to suffer from unrequited love!

She twisted her hair onto the top of her head and waded towards the beach. 'Good evening,' she said in English, deliberately using that language to distance herself from him.

He answered in the same tongue. 'Fili said you're going back to New Zealand with the new owner.'

'Where on earth did she get that idea?' Alli answered contemptuously, stooping to pick up her pareu.

'From Sisilu, I suppose.' His eyes were hot, but his voice revealed his pain. 'She said you'd talked about sleeping with him so he'd keep the resort open.'

Furious, Alli knotted her pareu over her scanty swimsuit. 'Slade Hawkings has the coldest eyes of anyone I've ever seen. I don't think he's open to negotiation.'

Tama gazed at her hungrily, his eyes sliding the length of the wet pareu. 'You want to go to New Zealand. He might take you.'

She drew a deep breath. 'Tama, be sensible.'

'Alli, marry me.' When she shook her head and started off up the beach he caught her up. 'I can change my father's mind. He knows you and loves you—he'll come around soon enough.'

The cluster of coconut palms beside the house was only a few metres away. Gently she said, 'Your father will never change his mind. The last thing he wants for you is marriage to a woman with no background, no family, no nothing. He is an aristocrat of the old school, and I'm a nobody. It simply won't happen.'

He grabbed her by the arm and swung her to face him. 'It could if you agreed.'

She said firmly, 'No. I'm going to New Zealand.'

'Why?'

She looked around at the glimmering expanse of the lagoon, the elegant statement of the coconut palms, the combination of soft sweetness and astringent salty scent that spelt Valanu to her—the sheer magical beauty of it all. Reverting to the local Polynesian tongue for emphasis, she said quietly, 'Because it's where I belong. Just as you belong here.'

He made a sound in his throat and pulled her against him. Startled, Alli stiffened, and when he began to press kisses over her face she mumbled, 'Let me go. Now!'

'Alli, you're driving me mad,' he said in a low, passionate voice. 'I need you—'

'No, you don't.' Instinctively repelled by his arousal, she had to remind herself that this was Tama, who'd teased her all through school, who'd laughed and picked her up when she'd fallen over, who'd been so like a brother that she hadn't even realised when he'd decided to fall in love with her.

He rested his cheek on her head. 'You don't know how I feel,' he muttered.

She freed her arms and cupped his face with both her hands, staring into his eyes and trying to convince him. He seemed older and harder, as though he'd made up his mind to do something.

'I know I don't feel the same way!' she said sadly.

'Because you won't let yourself—you think it's wrong because my parents are so old-fashioned. I can make you feel it.'

He pressed an urgent kiss on her mouth, and this time she pushed at his chest, her hand tightening over his solar plexus as she clenched her jaw. When she could speak she said, 'Tama, no!'

Something in her tone got to him, because he dragged in a deep breath and stepped back, dropping his arms. Tears stung her eyes as she watched him struggle for control.

Why on earth did this business between the sexes have to be so complicated?

He said thickly, 'I love you.'

'Tama, I think of you as my brother. Your mother is the only mother I've ever had,' she said gently. 'I love you too, but not like that.'

He looked away. 'We could make it impossible for them to say no,' he said unevenly. 'If there was a child my mother wouldn't turn it away.'

Alli sucked in her breath, but said steadily, 'You'd have to rape me, and you wouldn't do that.'

'No,' he said, and the hungry, determined man disappeared, replaced by the beloved companion of her childhood.

'And we couldn't do that to your parents,' she said, aching for him. 'They trust you—and they trust me too.'

He gathered his dignity around him to kiss her forehead softly. 'Then there is nothing more to be said. I hope your voyage brings you happiness, little sister.'

And he turned and strode away down the beach, leaving Alli shaken and forlorn, wrenched by the loss of her last security as she watched him disappear into the darkness. Slowly she turned and walked towards the house she'd grown up in, no longer a sanctuary for her.

Two steps away from the clump of coconut palms her every sense suddenly woke to full alert, pulling her skin tight in primal fear. She stopped and stared into the shadows. Tall and dark and dominating, a broad shoulder propped against a sinuous trunk, someone waited for her there, silent and still as some sleekly dangerous night predator.

Foreboding knotted her stomach, and her pulse ricocheted. In her most matter-of-fact tone, she said, 'Good evening, Mr Hawkings.'

He straightened, but stayed where he was. Illuminated by the gathering radiance of a rising moon, she felt exposed and vulnerable.

'Good evening, Alli.' There was a subtle insult in his use of her first name. 'I thought for a moment I might have to come to your rescue.'

'No,' she said curtly. 'Have you lost your way?'

'On the contrary. I came looking for you.'

A flash of fear hollowed out her stomach. Acutely aware of the way her pareu clung to her wet body, she asked huskily, 'Why?'

He paused. 'To see what a con artist looks like.'

The cold, implicit threat in his words silenced her until she produced enough composure to say, 'I don't know what you mean.'

'You wrote a letter to Marian Hawkings informing her you were her long-lost daughter and asking her why she abandoned you and your father.'

Sweat sheened her forehead and temples. Her heart skidded to a halt in her chest, then started up double time. She could only just discern the arrogant framework of his face, and what she saw there terrified her—icy distaste and a ruthless warning.

Alli swallowed to ease a throat suddenly dry. 'How—how did you know?'

'I'm glad you don't deny it. She told me.'

'Are you related to her?' she asked breathlessly.

'In a way.'

Frustration ate into her, but she rallied. 'I don't remember saying anything in my letter that could be construed as a con.'

'Perhaps blackmail would be a better word. I read your letter; it was aggressive, and there was a clear intimation that you were coming to New Zealand to meet her.' His voice was hard and uncompromising.

'I didn't intend it to be aggressive, but, yes, I said that. She owes me one meeting, surely?' Alli fought back a bewildering mixture of emotions. 'So she's not going to meet me?'

'Why should she? She has no daughter called Alli—'

'Alison,' she said raggedly.

'Or Alison.'

'Actually, it's Alison Marian.'

'Is it?' He couldn't have made his disbelief more obvious. Without bothering to comment, he went on, 'On the date you gave for your birth she was in Thailand on holiday with friends. I don't know where you got your information, Alli—always providing it wasn't just a stab in the dark—but she rejects it entirely.'

Pain squeezed Alli's heart in a vice so ferocious she thought she might never be able to take a breath again. She fought it with every ounce of will. 'I see,' she said, each word deep and deliberate and steady. 'In that case there's nothing more to be said. Goodbye, Mr Hawkings.'

'Not so fast. Where did you hear about her?'

It couldn't hurt to tell him. Perhaps it might even rock his confident self-possession a little. She'd like that—it might ease the pain that gripped her.

'I saw her name on my father's marriage certificate.'

He moved so quickly she gasped and took a stumbling step backwards. In the moonlight his face was a mask, superbly carved to reveal no emotion, but she saw the glitter of his eyes and knew with a bitter satisfaction that she had startled him.

'You're lying,' he said, and covered the ground between them in two quick strides.

Head held high and eyes glittering, she stood her ground. 'She was Marian Carter, born in Hampshire, England. She met my father there, married him a year later, and emigrated to New Zealand with him. I was born roughly two years afterwards. Not that it's any of your business.'

'I don't believe you,' he said icily.

'So?' Humiliated, she felt her wet hair tumble around her shoulders in a clammy mass. 'I'm not interested in what you believe. If Mrs Hawkings doesn't want to acknowledge me, I'm certainly not going to press the issue.' She gave him a brittle smile. 'Harassing one's own mother is not polite, after all.'

A lean, implacable hand clamped around the fine bones of her wrist. He didn't hurt her, but she felt like a bird caught in a trap.

'You're a cool one,' he said levelly.

It wasn't a compliment. Every cell in her body shrieked an alarm. 'Let me go.'

Moonlight gleamed on his face, lighting up a smile that chilled her with its cynicism. 'Who was the boy on the beach?' he enquired in a tone that combined both indolence and steel.

'An old friend.' She twisted away and stepped past him, aware that he chose to let her go. Although he hadn't marked her skin, his touch had scorched through her like lightning on a hilltop.

His smile narrowed. 'A pity your touching renunciation wasn't necessary.'

Alli looked up at him with apprehension tinged by fear. In spite of the fact that she disliked him intensely, he made her overwhelmingly conscious of the hard muscle under the superbly cut casual clothes, of the cutting edge of his intellect.

'Is eavesdropping a hobby of yours?' she asked, not trying to soften the scathing words.

She'd have said it was impossible, but the autocratic mask of his face hardened even further. 'Only when I can't avoid it. You should check that no one's around before you turn a man down,' he shot back, a raw note in his voice scuffing her nerves into shocking sensitivity.

They were quarrelling—yet she didn't know him enough to quarrel. 'I don't need to—the islanders are too courteous to intrude.'

'Or too accustomed to seeing you with a man to be interested?' he enquired pleasantly.

Her breathing became shallow; instinct warned her to get the hell out of there, but she couldn't move. Eyes widening, she stared up into his formidable face.

He lifted her chin with one forefinger and smiled as he examined her—feature by feature—with unsparing calculation.

Not a nice smile. Yet she couldn't move, couldn't do anything except suffer that inspection as though she was an object being examined with a view to purchase.

'It's no use casting your spells on me.' Each word was delivered with a flat lack of expression, although a contemptuous undertone sent wariness shivering down Alli's spine. 'Your mouth is slightly swollen from another man's kisses and I've always been foolishly fastidious. I'm also immune to the enchantment of a tropical moon and a pretty face.'

Ripples of feverish sensation threatening to carry her away, Alli gritted her teeth until she could say evenly, 'Goodnight.'

She straightened her shoulders and strode up the shell path towards the house without a backward glance. Yet she knew the exact second Slade Hawkings turned away and headed back down the beach towards the resort.

Because it hurt too much to think of her mother's rejection, she spent the hours until she slept vengefully imagining what she should have done when Slade touched her. Unfortunately imagining him sprawled on the sand clasping his midriff and gasping for breath proved to be an unsatisfactory substitute for the real thing. Why hadn't she let him know bluntly that she resented strangers pawing her?

Instead of hitting him, she'd noticed the tiny pulse beating in his jaw, registered the elusive fragrance that was Slade Hawkings's alone, and felt the fierce demand of his will-power battering her defences.

She found some relief in punching her pillow before turning over to listen to the waves on the reef. Always before their pounding had soothed her, but tonight unwilling excitement still throbbed like a drug through her veins and, later, through her dreams.

Alli made sure she arrived at work ahead of time the next morning. After restocking the shelves she arranged a cluster of brazenly gold hibiscus on the counter, their elaborate frills reminding her of the frothy confections Edwardian society women had worn on their proudly poised heads.

'Good morning,' Barry Simcox said from behind her.

Pulse hammering, she straightened and whirled in one smooth movement.

He stared at her in bewilderment. 'Are you all right?'

Feeling an idiot, she muttered, 'I'm fine, thank you. You surprised me.'

'I didn't realise you were the nervous type.'

'I'm not!' she said truthfully, smiling to show him that she was completely in control of her erratic responses.

He nodded, and looked around the shop. 'You do have a knack with design,' he said absently. 'Hawkings mentioned it yesterday.'

'Did he?' She wanted to ask him what else the new owner had said, but of course she didn't. Instead she probed tentatively, 'Has he told you anything about his plans for Sea Winds?'

His pleasant mouth turned down at the corners. 'Nothing. He's playing his cards damned close to his chest.'

Like her and the rest of the staff, Barry stood to lose his job if the resort was abandoned. However, he could go back to Australia and resume his career.

She summoned a bright smile. 'A woman yesterday said we ought to mass-produce the quilts. She thought we should import some sewing machines and set up a little factory.' Her laughter blended with his startled guffaw. 'I didn't tell her that most of the islanders have sewing machines, or explain that the reason the quilts are so valuable is that they're handmade.'

A cold voice said, 'If you're ready, Simcox, I'll see you now.'

Poor Barry almost choked. 'Yes, sure, certainly,' he said, turning away from Alli so quickly he had to grab the nearest thing, which happened to be her bare shoulder.

'Sorry,' he babbled, letting her go as though her skin had burnt his fingers.

Keeping her eyes away from Slade Hawkings, Alli retired behind the counter and opened the till.

'Good morning, Alli,' he said, the thread of mockery through his words telling her that he understood her reaction and found it amusing.

Her eyes glinted beneath her lashes. 'Good morning, Mr Hawkings,' she returned with every ounce of sweetness she could summon, ignoring Barry's alarmed stare.

'You're looking a little tired,' Slade said, adding, 'Perhaps you should try to get to bed earlier?'

Although she read the warning in the manager's expression, she showed her teeth anyway. 'You needn't worry. I won't let anything I do at night affect my work.'

She heard the hiss of Barry's breath whistling past his teeth. Far too heartily, he leapt in with, 'Slade, I've got those figures ready for you now.'

Slade Hawkings looked at him as though he was an irritating insect. 'Let's see them, then.'

Watching them walk back across the foyer in the direction of the one suite the resort boasted—which Slade had claimed—Alli wondered how two men, from the back rather similar in size and height, could look so different. Barry walked straight enough, and his clothes were good, yet beside the other man he looked…well, spectacularly insignificant.

Everything about Slade Hawkings proclaimed that he was completely in command of himself, his surroundings and his life. He looked, Alli thought with a sudden clutch of panic, exactly like a man who'd close down a poorly performing resort without a hint of compassion for the people who worked there.

So why did her body respond with swift, forbidden excitement whenever she saw him?

For the next two days rumours buzzed around the resort, growing wilder and more depressing each hour. Alli was kept busy with a new wave of tourists, most of whom wandered into the souvenir shop at some time to stock up on T-shirts, bright cotton pareus, or a hat for protection from the fierce sun. Excited children raced past the shop on their way to the lagoon, and each night the troupe danced and sang as though their lives depended on it.

'Barry's looking pretty sick, and the waiter who delivers the meals says the Big Man is getting grimmer and grimmer,' Sisilu said from the depths of an elderly cane chair on the second night.

She'd called in on her way home after the floorshow, joining Alli on the verandah.

'What's Hawkings doing?'

'Going over figures.' Sisilu could never be serious for long, and almost immediately she started to laugh. 'Hey, did anyone tell you about the girl who thought Mr Hawkings was part of the package that first night?'

Alli's brows shot up. 'No! What happened?'

'She saw him at the show and really came on to him.'

'What did he do?'

Sisilu grinned. 'He joined her group, and half an hour later he'd fixed her up with a good-looking American. Fili said she looked like a stunned fish, trying to work out what had happened! He's clever, that man.' She sent Alli a laughing sideways glance. 'So what's with you and him?'

'Nothing,' Alli shot back.

'Fili said the Big Man saw you and Barry laughing together in the shop and didn't like it.'

'Fili must spend all her time dodging round looking for scandal,' Alli said, resigned to the fact that on an island the size of Valanu nothing was secret. 'And when she doesn't find it she makes it up. If Slade Hawkings looked angry it's because he doesn't like me and I don't like him.'

Sisilu chuckled. 'So why doesn't he like you?'

'Oh—we just rub each other up the wrong way.' Alli wished she'd kept her mouth shut.

'Which usually means that there's something going on underneath. I think he wants you, and men like that are used to taking what they want.'

A hot little thrill ran through Alli, but she said, 'You've got an over-active imagination.'

'I saw him watch you walk across the beach yesterday.' Sisulu fanned herself and rolled her eyes. 'His face didn't change, but I could feel his attention like laser beams. I'm surprised you didn't.'

Alli moved uncomfortably and Sisilu started to laugh. 'You did, didn't you? I can tell you did! You going to do something about it?'

CHAPTER THREE

ALLI shook her head so swiftly the orchid behind her left ear went flying into the scented night. 'Even if he does, I don't know anything about…well, about anything. You know what my father was like.'

'He didn't do you any favours,' Sisilu said, wrinkling her forehead as she recalled Ian Pierce's strictness. 'Making love's nothing much—I mean, it's great, and I like doing it, but the world doesn't revolve around it. The longer you put it off the bigger and bigger it gets, I suppose. Are you scared?'

'Not exactly,' Alli said thoughtfully.

When Tama had kissed her she'd felt nothing beyond regret that she couldn't feel as he so obviously did. But Slade's touch had charged her with forbidden excitement. She could still feel it like fireworks inside, all flash and fire and heat.

Hastily she finished, 'But I feel that if my father thought it was so important then I shouldn't do it just for fun.'

Sisilu understood respect for one's elders. She shrugged, then cocked her head and got to her feet as laughter floated through the sultry air. 'Sounds like Fili and the others going home; I'll go with them.'

After she'd left Alli got ready for bed, but an unusual restlessness drove her outside again. She stood on the edge of the verandah and gazed around, wondering if she'd hate New Zealand, as Sisilu so confidently expected.

She'd certainly miss the moonlight glimmering on the still surface of the lagoon, and the breeze rustling the palm fronds, carrying the tang of salt and the tropical ripeness of flowers and fruit. And she'd miss her friends.

But she was going, whatever she missed.

She sat down on the old swing seat and rocked rhythmically. What exactly was Slade up to? Why had he bought the resort in the first place? It seemed an odd thing for a hard-nosed businessman to do. Surely he'd checked the figures before he'd paid a cent for it? He must have known that it was perilously close to failure.

Her mouth curved cynically. And he certainly didn't strike her as a philanthropist, ready to sink his own money into a dying enterprise just to help the islanders!

If he did close Sea Winds she didn't know what she'd do. She'd have nothing—no future, no present, no chance or choice. The island had a policy of jobs for native Valanuans, and she didn't want to take any work from them. In fact, she'd been training someone to take over in the souvenir shop.

Her father's income had died with him; even the house was hers only because the tribal council let her stay there as a mark of respect to her father.

Besides, there was Tama...

The crunch of shells beneath shoes brought her to her feet; heart beating feverishly, she peered into the darkness. Even before her eyes made out the man strolling up the shell path from the beach she knew who he was.

Fighting back a heady excitement that blasted out of nowhere, she blurted, 'What do you want?'

'To talk to you,' Slade Hawkings said coolly, taking the steps. He stopped at the edge of the verandah, his silhouette blocking out stars and the moonpath over the lagoon.

Dwarfed by his formidable presence, Alli asked abruptly, 'What about?' Oh, Lord, she sounded like a belligerent teenager.

'The resort.'

'Why?' she said warily, brain racing. 'I don't know anything about its financial affairs.'

'Simcox tells me that you're very well integrated into Valanuan life.'

She stiffened. Where was this going? 'I can't remember any other home.'

'But it's not your home,' he pointed out. 'You have a New Zealand passport.'

'What has that got to do with Sea Winds?'

He turned to examine the garden. 'I believe your father leased the house from his local tribal council.'

Chills chased each other across her skin. She said pleasantly, 'You've been doing some research. Why?'

'I make it my policy to learn as much as I can about my enemies,' he said calmly, turning back to look at her.

To cover her shocked gasp she rushed into speech. 'I suppose I should be terrified to be an enemy of the great Slade Hawkings? If I'd known that was a possibility I might not have written to my mother—'

'She isn't your mother,' he interrupted in a flat,

uncompromising tone. 'And you're right. I make a bad enemy.' He paused to let that sink in. 'However, I can be a good friend.'

But not to me, she thought, suspicion snaking through her.

'Above all, I'm a businessman.' Another deliberate pause.

As a technique for unsettling people, Alli thought, trying to hide her growing unease with flippancy, it worked brilliantly. She didn't know whether he was trying to provoke her into speech, but common sense warned her that silence was by far the best option.

He said matter-of-factly, 'You know that Sea Winds is losing money hand over fist; I'd be a lousy businessman if I let such a bad investment drag my profits down year after year.'

This time Alli couldn't hold back her biting comment. 'I'm surprised a businessman of your reputation bought the place.'

'I had reasons,' he said shortly, a note of warning in the deep voice.

What reasons? The whisper of an implication smoked across her brain, only to be dismissed. Sinking though it was, Sea Winds would have cost him a lot of money—far more than he'd have needed to spend if he wanted to gain power over her.

Alli lifted her gaze to his dark silhouette. Against the radiance of the moon she saw a profile etched from steel, and shivered inwardly. Something Sisilu had said to her came back again—something like *be nice to him—for all of us*...

Her teeth worried her lip before she said neutrally, 'If you spent money on it—'

'Surprisingly enough, money isn't always the answer. It should never have been built here. There isn't room for a decent airport so everything has to come through Sant'Rosa, and the civil war there has made tourists extremely wary of this part of the world.'

Everything he said in that aloof, dispassionate voice was the truth, yet the conversation rang oddly false. Alli swallowed. 'Why are you telling me this?'

'I want your opinion on what closing the resort will do to the islanders.'

'Why me?' She didn't try to hide her incredulity.

He shrugged. 'I'm not stupid. You know these people, and I'm willing to accept that you want to do your best for your friends.'

'Even though I'm a blackmailer?' she flashed back.

'I assume that even blackmailers have friends.' His tone could have cut ice. 'You seem to.'

It had been stupid to let him see how his opinion of her stung. Compared to the welfare of the islanders, her hurt feelings were totally unimportant.

She drew in a deep breath and said frankly, 'Most of them will go back to working copra, planting and fishing and village life. The tribal council won't have as much money for schooling, because copra is not hugely profitable, so the secondary school will almost certainly close. Bright children won't be able to go to university. The health clinic will probably close too, except for tours by visiting doctors.' She couldn't see his expression, but he could see hers when she finished bluntly, 'Some people will certainly die.'

His silence lifted the hairs on the back of her neck. Should she have pleaded? Did he have any sort of social conscience at all, or was this a trick?

Eventually he said, 'So what would *you* do to keep the resort open?'

Panic kicked her in the stomach. 'I—what? What could I do?'

He walked across the verandah, stopping so close to her she could see the white flash of his narrow smile.

'Keeping Sea Winds going would be a sacrifice for me—I'm asking what you're prepared to sacrifice for your friends.'

Blood pumped through her, awakening her body to urgent life, but her brain seemed to have been overwhelmed by lethargy. She moistened her lips and croaked, 'If you mean what I think you're meaning...'

'That's exactly what I mean,' he said, that note of ironic amusement more pronounced. 'I want you, Alli. You must have guessed—it's not as though you're a sweet little innocent.'

Stunned, she licked her lips and swallowed. 'You're going to have to be clearer than that.'

Boredom descended like a mask over his face. 'Really?' he mocked, his mouth twisting. 'Then perhaps I should demonstrate.'

And he kissed her.

Alli had read books, she'd listened to friends discussing their love life—and she'd been kissed often enough to know what it was all about. But until Slade's mouth took hers she'd had no idea that a man's kiss could drive every sensible thought ahead of it like leaves in a hurricane, robbing her of breath and common sense until she was left witless and shaking in his arms.

His mouth was cool and masterful, and potent as

lightning, she thought vaguely, before a rush of sensation blotted out everything but wildly primitive need.

When he broke the kiss her hands tightened on the fine cotton of his shirt and she pressed closer with an instinctively sinuous movement, afraid that he'd walk away and leave her.

'Sweet,' he said, his voice raw with sensual arousal. 'Open your mouth for me...'

Sighing, she said his name, and he laughed beneath his breath and kissed her again. And this time there was nothing cool about it at all.

Locked against his hardening body, she shuddered as her passionate response rocketed her into another universe. Desire merged inevitably into hunger, then blossomed into a desperate craving. This, she thought dimly as he explored the soft inner parts of her mouth, as she savoured the exotic taste of him, as she melted into surrender—this was what she had been waiting for...

Slade lifted his head, but only to kiss her eyelids. Strong arms tightened across her back, pulling her against him. Shudders of pleasure ran like rills through her. She moved languorously against him, and shivered at the fierce delight the heat and pressure of his taut body kindled in the pit of her stomach.

She felt his chest expand, and was filled with excitement because she was doing this to him.

No wonder her father had kept such a close watch on her—this was dangerously addictive, a reckless abandonment to sensuous thrills.

And then Slade's arms dropped and he stepped back, leaving her shivering in the warm night air, her body filled with frustrated longing for something she'd never experienced.

'Just so we don't get this wrong,' he said evenly, as though nothing at all had happened, 'are you offering me yourself in return for my keeping Sea Winds open?'

Humiliation doused every last bit of arousal. Cold and furious, Alli clenched her hands by her sides to stop herself from shaking. 'Is that what you want?'

'I'm always prepared to deal,' he said, watching her with half-closed eyes.

'No,' she said when she could speak again. 'I'm no prostitute.'

He wielded silence like a weapon, but two could play at that game. Fighting back tears of shock, she refused to let loose the bitter words that trembled on her tongue.

'I wasn't thinking of prostitution,' he said obliquely. 'More an exchange of benefits.'

'A business deal?' She didn't have to summon the scorn in her voice—it came without warning. 'But that's what prostitution is, surely? There's certainly no emotion in it.'

He smiled without humour and touched the corner of her mouth with a knuckle. 'Really?' he drawled, tracing its lush, tender contours. 'You could have fooled me. Shall I kiss you again?'

Something unravelled deep inside her. Aching with desolation, she stepped back, away from his knowledgeable, tormenting caress, and said stonily, 'There's a difference between sensation and emotion.'

'I think we could probably forget about semantics while we made love.'

The best way to finish this would be to prove how utterly stupid she'd been. 'So let's deal. How often would you expect me to sleep with you in return for the continuation of the resort? Just once? Or would you expect me to be available whenever you came to Valanu? How often would that be?'

'Whenever I wanted,' he said with a silky lack of emphasis. 'I don't think just once would slake either of us.'

'And how long would it last?'

'Until I got tired of you,' he said coolly. 'Of course I'd expect you to be faithful in between visits.'

'And would you be faithful?' When he paused she looked straight up into his face and said, in a voice that shook with scorn, 'Nothing would persuade me to sleep with you for money, or benefits, or any other reason. In fact, I don't ever want to see you again.'

'That can certainly be arranged,' he said.

She was wincing at the sheer off-hand brutality of his reply when he began again, and this time the sexual edge was gone from his tone.

Brisk, businesslike, without inflection, he said, 'Get down off your high horse, Alli—I don't want you in my bed. However, I'll keep the resort going if you stay here on the island and work in the souvenir shop.'

'What?' she whispered incredulously.

'You heard.' His voice hardened. 'If you agree, your friends will keep their jobs, children will go on to university, and people will live.'

'Why?' But she knew why.

'It's a simple transaction. I don't want you contacting or trying to see Marian Hawkings ever again.'

Hearing it like that—a bald statement delivered in a tone that brooked no compromise—sent equal parts of anger and desolation surging through her.

'And you have the nerve to call me a blackmailer,' she said flatly.

'So we each use the weapons we have to hand,' he retorted with bland indifference.

Even as she admitted to herself that she had no choice, she looked for a way out. 'And do I have to stay here for the rest of my life—or Marian Hawkings's life?'

He paused, then said, 'You'll leave Valanu when I agree you can.'

Fear and frustration almost made her burst into a furious outburst, but if she lost control he might renege on the deal. She said wearily, 'Why are you doing this?'

He misunderstood her, perhaps deliberately. 'Because I want you kept well away from Marian.'

'If I promise not to contact her—'

He lifted a hand, but when she shrank back he dropped it again, saying incredulously, 'I wasn't going to hit you!'

'I know.' She'd realised that the second she'd jumped back.

'Did your father beat you?' he asked in a soft, lethal tone that scared her more than anything else.

'No—never!' Anger drove her to say, 'He was a gentleman—literally!' She let the word sizzle through the air before finishing woodenly, 'All right, I'll accept your offer—but I want it in writing first.'

She was shocked when he laughed, apparently with

real amusement. Mortified, she heard him say, 'You'll hear from my lawyers within a week.'

'If I don't, the deal's off,' she said rashly. 'And for your—and Marian Hawkings's—information, I had no intention of forcing myself onto the woman. I just wanted to ask her some questions.'

'Then learn to couch your letters in more diplomatic language,' he returned curtly, turning to go. 'As for your questions—she has no answers. If this whole business about looking for your mother is true, you've been searching up the wrong street.'

It took a real effort, but Alli kept her silence. She knew that Marian Hawkings was her mother, but the lies the woman must have told Slade fitted in with the profile she'd built in her mind—a woman who had never wanted anything to do with the daughter she'd borne.

She said, 'Before you go, tell me one thing.'

In a voice that conveyed both a warning and a threat, he said, 'I don't have to tell you anything.' But he stopped at the foot of the steps and turned to look at her.

Refusing to be denied, Alli ploughed on. 'This is going to cost you a huge amount of money, so what is Marian Hawkings to you? I know she's not your mother—unless you were the result of an affair before she married your father. I assume she's your stepmother.'

For a moment she thought he was going to refuse to answer, until he said, 'She is my stepmother. Now I want an answer from you—you said that you saw her name on your father's marriage certificate. She was married before she married my father, but her first husband's name was not Ian Pierce.'

'I know,' she said quietly. 'It was Hugo Greville. Hugo Ian Greville—Pierce was my father's mother's maiden name. He changed his name by deed poll when your stepmother left him. After he died, I found the papers with their marriage certificate, the divorce papers, and a clipping about her marriage to your father.'

Moonlight lovingly delineated his features, the silver flood dwelling on the strength and cold determination that stamped his face. 'So you knew who I was before I got here?'

'No,' she said acidly. 'You weren't mentioned in the newspaper clipping. And I had no idea the new owner of Sea Winds was another Hawkings.' She looked at him to see if he believed her, but his expression revealed nothing. 'Even when you got here I didn't make the connection. It is a reasonably common name.'

'I see.' He was silent for several seconds. 'I'm on my way out of Valanu in half an hour. Keep your nose clean and you might win some time off for good behaviour.'

Bewildered, furious and exhausted, Alli watched him stride towards the beach until the shadows swallowed him up.

CHAPTER FOUR

ALLI swung a long leg over the horse's back and dropped gracefully from the saddle. 'Good girl,' she said, chirruping in a way the grey understood. It gave a soft whicker when she flipped the reins and stood looking along the beach, north, to where Valanu lay, thousands of kilometres away across the lonely Pacific.

Eighteen months after she'd made that bargain with Slade Hawkings she'd waved the island a tear-drenched farewell. Although she still missed her friends there, after six months in New Zealand she was becoming accustomed to its temperate climate, was enjoying the play of seasons and the new life she'd made for herself.

And, although today was chilly, the Maori celebration of Matariki had long passed, with the rising of the Pleiades in the northern sky. Spring was almost over and summer was on its way.

'Hey, Alli!'

She turned to wave to the middle-aged man loping across the short grass of the paddock, bald head gleaming.

'Hi, Joe! Trouble?'

'Might be. You've got a visitor.' He extended his hand for the reins. 'I'll deal with Lady and you go on down to the Lodge; the guy doesn't look as though he's used to being kept waiting.'

Alli frowned, keeping hold of the reins. 'Who is it?'

'Come on, hand 'em over. He didn't say who he was, just that he wanted to see you.' He grinned. 'Perhaps he saw your photo in the paper when you helped rescue those yachties, and realised that under all that salt and sand there was a pretty face.'

'I hope not,' she said involuntarily.

She'd been desperate to keep out of the limelight, but a persistent journalist had managed to get one shot of her hauling on the line that had brought the crew of the yacht to safety through the huge surf.

At least her face had been barely recognisable. The other staff at the Lodge had joked that the only reason the shot had appeared in the paper was because she'd dumped her wet jeans when they'd dragged her down in the surf, and the tights beneath showed her legs to perfection.

When she still hadn't moved, Joe jerked his head towards the backpackers' lodge and said, 'Go on. If he gets stroppy yell for Tui.'

She laughed. Joe's wife was built on sturdy lines, a woman with a tongue that could slice skin, yet sing tenderly haunting lullabies to her grandchildren. Sometimes she joked that she needed to do both with the backpackers who came to this stretch of coastline to surf the massive waves.

'Thanks,' Alli said, and set off along the narrow metalled race that led through the dunes to the Lodge.

Who on earth could her visitor be? The friends she'd made all lived around the Lodge, yet if Joe didn't know who he was the man couldn't be a local.

Perhaps it was someone from Valanu?

She stepped through the door into the reception area and said, 'Sorry I took so long to get—'

Shock drove the breath from her lungs and the words froze on her tongue.

'I'm a patient man,' Slade Hawkings said calmly, turning around from his scrutiny of the scenic calendar on the wall.

Two years faded into nothingness and she felt as defenceless against his powerful male magnetism as she had when they'd first met. He was watching her with the aloof, unreadable expression she recalled so well.

She swallowed and asked thinly, 'What do you want?'

He cocked an arrogant black brow. 'Perhaps to see why you reneged on our deal.'

'I haven't contacted m—Marian Hawkings,' she shot back. 'Which is what the deal was really about.'

'That's a matter of opinion.' But he spoke without rancour and some of her apprehension faded.

'And the Valanu resort is no longer losing money,' she finished.

'Thanks, I believe, largely to you.' Lashes drooped over the hard green eyes, so startling in his tanned face. 'Who'd have thought that a little South Seas siren would turn into a hot publicist?'

'How did you know—?' She stopped abruptly. *'Siren?'*

'If it fits,' Slade drawled. 'When ideas for improving the hotel's publicity started to percolate through, the new manager had to admit they came from you. Targeting the upper end of the market and laying on a flying boat to get the guests in from Sant'Rosa was an inspired move. The nostalgia angle is working very well, and lunch on an uninhabited island seems to be appealing to plenty of would-be Robinson Crusoes out there.'

She shrugged. 'Well, those who are filthy rich, anyway. I was surprised your organisation ran with my ideas.'

'They were fresh,' he said indifferently, 'and it was clear that you had the backing of the chief.'

She had to stop herself from looking as uncomfortable as she felt. Tama's father had packed his son off to Auckland, ostensibly to take a degree but really to get him away from his unsuitable crush on Alli, who had, as the chief said, behaved properly. In return, he'd pragmatically thrown his considerable prestige and authority behind her plans for the resort.

And the new manager, who'd arrived two days after Slade left, and a week before Barry Simcox went back to Australia, had let her have her head.

Slade continued smoothly, 'Tell me, did Barry get back together with his wife once he landed in Australia?'

Something in his tone made her narrow her eyes, but he met her enquiring look with an opaque, unreadable gaze.

Alli shrugged. 'How would I know?'

He looked amused, but said easily, 'How did you get off Valanu? The manager said no one seemed to know where you were until they got a postcard from Fiji a week or so later.'

She said stiffly, 'If he'd thought to ask the chief he'd have found out. I worked my passage on a yacht.'

'I suspected so.' His smile showed a few too many teeth. 'The one with the group of young Australians?'

'The one with the middle-aged Alaskan couple,' she snapped.

His brows rose in a manner she found infuriating, but he said blandly, 'I suppose I should be grateful that before you left you trained someone to take your place in the souvenir shop.'

'I don't want your gratitude,' she returned. 'What are you doing here? And don't tell me you're going to force me back to Valanu. I didn't know how to deal with that sort of blackmail before—but I do now.'

'I'm pleased to hear it. No, I'm not ordering you back. I have no power to make you go, and I rarely repeat myself. And, as you said, the whole idea was to keep you away from Marian.' His demeanour changed from indolent assurance to one of decisiveness. 'But now she wants to see you.'

She said quietly, 'I don't want to see her.'

Slade waited for a long moment, his expression intimidating. When he spoke his voice was a lethal purr. 'A little revenge, Alli?'

'Alison,' she told him. 'I call myself Alison now— more adult, don't you think?' She still hadn't got used to it, though.

'Your employer called you Alli.'

She said curtly, 'He shortens everyone's name. And, no, it's not revenge.'

'Then what is it?'

Alli paused, trying to work out how she felt. Longing to see her mother vied with another instinct. 'Self-defence. I can only take so much rejection. And so far that's all she's done to me.'

In the intimidating, angular set of his face she saw the man who'd expanded the thriving firm he'd inherited from his father to a pre-eminent position on the world stage.

He said smoothly, 'I don't think rejection is what she has in mind.'

The desire to meet Marian Hawkings tempted Alli so strongly it almost overwhelmed her common sense. If she didn't take this opportunity she might never have another. And eventually she'd despise herself for sheltering behind the cowardly fear of being hurt. But caution drove her to probe, 'Then what *does* she have in mind?' Acceptance would be too much to hope for.

Slade wondered what was going on behind her guarded face. 'I don't know,' he said abruptly.

She looked at him with those exotic lion eyes. 'How did you find me?'

'The newspaper photograph.'

Her dark brows lifted in irony. 'That was a month or so ago.'

'Marian's been ill,' he said shortly.

Once he'd given Marian the dossier his investigator had put together she'd avoided the subject for several weeks. Then a bout of flu had laid her low, just after he'd seen the photograph of Alli in the newspaper.

It still irritated the hell out of him that, in spite of the grainy photograph, her face had leapt out at him from the page.

Not that she was classically beautiful, he thought critically, angered by the weakness that tested his self-control. But something about her challenging eyes and inviting, sensuous mouth stirred his sexuality into prowling appreciation, aided by the rare combination of dark, rich hair and glowing golden skin, and the body her lovers had woken to lush, svelte femininity.

When Marian had decided she wanted to find Alli he'd had to admit that he knew where she was, although he'd refused to contact her until the doctor had agreed that Marian was fit enough to cope.

He said abruptly, 'She wants to tell you something.'

Hope, so long repressed, flickered like a spark inside her. 'If it's just that she's not my mother she's already told me that, remember?'

His broad shoulders moved in a slight shrug. 'It's not that.'

'Then what?'

He walked across to the window and looked beyond the garden to the regenerating sand dunes, replanted with the native grass that had been the original vegetation. 'It isn't mine to tell,' he said curtly.

'I can't just leave the Lodge.' Her quiet tone hid a desperate hunger to see the woman who'd given her life.

'I've already talked to your boss.'

'Joe?'

He smiled. 'His wife. She's giving you the rest of the afternoon off, and I believe you're not working tomorrow. I'll drive you down and make sure you get back.'

Alli fought a brief, vicious battle with herself before yielding to temptation. 'All right, I'll get changed.'

'Take enough clothes for the night.'

Her incredulous glance met eyes as cool and un-yielding as jade. 'I won't need them, surely?'

'Nevertheless, bring them.' When she looked mutinous he said matter-of-factly, 'I always believe in being prepared for any eventuality.'

Alli bit her lip, but when she came down twenty minutes later she carried a bag packed with a change of clothes.

She followed the sound of laughter to the kitchen, where Slade was drinking coffee and talking to Tui as she kneaded a batch of bread.

He seemed perfectly at home, and her employer was certainly enjoying his company, although that didn't stop her from saying firmly, 'Better give me your address and phone number in case I need to ring Alli up.'

Slade took out a slim black case and scribbled something on a business card. 'I've put my e-mail address there as well,' he said, anchoring the card to the table with a sugar bowl. 'Sometimes it's the quickest way to get in touch with me.'

A look of sheer horror settled on Tui's face. 'I'm not touching any computer,' she said robustly, dividing the dough into loaves. 'Alli keeps trying to make me use it, but it's just like magic to me, and I've always been a bit wary of magic.'

'According to you the telephone is magic too,' Alli teased, 'and so is electricity.'

'I understand those,' her boss told her, 'because I learnt about them at school. You young things can deal with the latest technology—I'll stick to my generation's.'

Insensibly warmed by the older woman's cheerfulness, Alli dropped a kiss on her cheek and went out with Slade Hawkings into the unknown.

Once in the large car, she sat back in a divinely comfortable seat, with the scent of leather in her nostrils, and watched the green landscape sweep by until apprehension seeped in to replace the lingering warmth of Tui's presence.

If she turned her head a little she could see Slade's hands on the wheel; for some stupid reason the sight of his lean, competent fingers made her heart quiver, so she kept her eyes on the lush countryside.

As though he understood her wariness, he began to talk—at first about the rescue of the yacht. When they'd exhausted that subject, somehow they segued onto the subject of books. He had definite views, some of which she agreed with and some she didn't. Alli discovered that he was that rare thing, a person who didn't take disagreement personally, and halfway to Auckland she realised that she was in the middle of a vigorous debate about a film she had enjoyed.

'Weak in both plot and acting,' he condemned, 'and with a dubious moral base.'

'Moral base?' she spluttered.

He shrugged. 'I subscribe to the usual moral values.'

Astonished, she lost the thread of her rejoinder and stared at his profile, the strong framework of his face providing a potent authority that would last him a lifetime. Heat smouldered in the pit of her stomach. The two years since she'd seen him had only increased her susceptibility to his disturbing magnetism.

Her silence brought a slanting ice-green glance.

'Cat got your tongue?' he asked politely, before returning his gaze to the road ahead.

She plunged back into the argument, but tension more complex than the merely sexual plucked at her nerves. She didn't want to like him; she certainly didn't want to feel this reluctant respect. It was far too dangerous.

The conversation lapsed as they approached Auckland and the traffic got heavier. Alli knew the route to the airport, and a few other necessary addresses, but once he left the motorway on one of the inner-city interchanges she lost all sense of where they were going.

It turned out to be one of Auckland's expensive eastern suburbs. Slade drove into the grounds of a modern block of apartments, parked in the visitors' car park and killed the engine, his face set in forbidding lines.

'She's expecting us,' he said.

Bewildering fear hollowed out Alli's stomach. Her mouth dry, she walked past camellia bushes and a graceful maple tree to the door, waiting while he pressed a button that activated a hidden microphone.

'Slade,' he said, adding, 'With a visitor.'

A woman—surely too young to be Marian Hawkings?—answered, 'Come on up.'

He opened the security door and said without expression, 'Marian's goddaughter is staying with her.'

Inside was discreetly luxurious—a bronze statue of vaguely Greek ancestry, a sea of carpet and marble, landscapes on the walls, a huge vase of flowers that only the closest observation revealed to be real.

'The lift is over here,' Slade said, his fingers resting

for one searing moment on her elbow as he indicated the elevator.

It delivered them too swiftly to the fourth floor, and more carpet that clung to Alli's shoes, more statuary, more flowers.

Trying to inject some stiffness into her backbone, she told herself grimly that Marian had landed on her feet after she left the man who'd changed his name to Ian Pierce.

The woman who opened the door was a few years older than Alli, elegant and beautiful. And every black hair of her head, every inch of white skin, radiated disapproval when she looked at Alli.

'Caroline, this is Alison Pierce,' Slade said. 'Alli, Caroline Forsythe, who has given up her holidays to stay with Marian while she's convalescing.'

'How do you do?' Caroline Forsythe didn't offer her hand. Her blue eyes skimmed Alli's face with a kind of wonder. 'It's no hardship to stay with Marian. Come on in—she's expecting you both.' She directed a brief, conspiratorial smile at Slade that spoke volumes. 'She's in the sitting room.'

Masochist, Alli thought fiercely, letting her anger overcome a faint, cold whisper of danger.

In the sitting room Alli vaguely registered light streaming in through large windows, gleaming on polished furniture, on more pictures in sophisticated colours, on flowers that blended with the décor.

A woman in a chair stood up. Her eyes met Alli's and the colour vanished from her skin, leaving it paper-white.

Horrified, Alli saw her crumple. She cried out, barely aware of Slade's swift, silent rush to catch

Marian Hawkings's fragile figure before she hit the floor.

As he lifted her in his arms Caroline hissed at Alli, 'Get out of here—*now*. Before she comes to, I want you out of this building.'

Blindly Alli turned away, but the whiplash of Slade's voice froze her. 'Caroline, get a glass of water with a splash of brandy in it,' he commanded, laying his burden down on the sofa, 'and make tea. Alli, stay where you are! She asked to meet you.'

Alli felt Caroline's dislike scorch through her. She didn't blame her; horrifying scenarios of her conception were blasting through her mind. The one thing she hadn't thought of was rape—but even now she simply couldn't conceive of her father doing that. After all, they'd been married...

'Sit down,' Slade went on, examining her with merciless eyes. 'I don't want you fainting too—you're as white as paper.'

She dropped into a chair, watching her mother's colourless face until Caroline came in with a glass and stood between them.

'It's all right, Marian,' Slade said gently. 'You fainted, that's all. You're fine now.'

'What—? Oh...' Marian Hawkings tried to struggle up.

'Lift your head a bit and drink this,' he said. 'I wouldn't have brought her if I'd known you were going to scare the hell out of us like that.'

'Let me see her.' But her voice was filled with dread.

'After you've had some of this.' He held the glass to her lips, only straightening when she'd taken several sips. He turned and with unyielding composure said to Alli, 'Come here.'

When Caroline started to object, Slade overrode her with one brief, intimidating glance.

'Alli?'

Slowly, skirting the furniture with extreme care, Alli made her way to the sofa, concern almost overriding her shock. The woman who lay there was still beautiful, with fine features and blue, blue eyes.

And after one swift, shaken glance Marian Hawkings went even whiter, and closed her eyes as though she'd seen something hideous.

With obvious effort she opened them again. 'Yes, I see. Caroline, my dear, do you mind leaving us? I'm sorry, but I need to speak to Alli and Slade alone.'

'Of course I don't mind,' the other woman said pleasantly, 'but do take care, Marian. You're not well yet.'

When she'd gone, Marian said weakly, 'Flu, that's all it was. Slade, would you help me up, please?'

He lifted her, propping her against the side and back of the sofa.

She looked at Alli, her eyes darkening. 'I wish I could say I was your mother, Alison, but I'm not.'

It was almost a relief. 'Then who was?' Alli asked in a cracked voice.

Marian swallowed, her face inexpressibly sad, and tried to speak. She whispered, 'I can't. Slade— please…'

Lying her back against the sofa, Slade said harshly, 'Your mother was Marian's sister.'

Nausea clutched Alli as the implication struck

home. She sprang to her feet, saying contemptuously, 'I don't believe it.'

'It happens,' he said briefly. He lifted a photograph from the side table and handed it to her. 'Your mother. And a copy of your birth certificate.' He paused before adding, 'Which you must have seen, as you have a passport.'

'My father organised it when I was sixteen,' she said absently. Now that she was faced with the proof she'd sought with such angry tenacity she didn't dare open the envelope.

Slowly, her fingers trembling, she slid the photograph free. Yes, there was her father, his expression almost anguished as he looked into a face—oh, God—into a face so like hers it gave her gooseflesh.

The woman in her father's arms was shorter than she was, but she had the same features—the same tilted eyes, the same exotic cheekbones, the same full mouth. She was laughing and her confidence blazed forth like a beacon, defiantly provocative.

A piece of paper beneath the photograph rustled in Alli's hand. She looked at it and swallowed. For the first time she saw her birth certificate, and on it her mother's name: Alison Carter. She had been twenty-four when she'd borne her lover's child.

Cold ripples of shock ran across Alli's skin. Whatever sins Alison had committed, she must have loved Marian to give her child her sister's name.

But to betray her like that! Sickened, she stared at the betraying document. Oh, God, her demands for acknowledgement must have opened up bitter humiliation and pain in this woman who was her aunt.

'What happened to her?' she asked in a raw voice.

Marian Hawkings looked at Slade. He said levelly, 'When Marian discovered that her sister was pregnant she told Hugo to leave. He did so, and the guilty lovers disappeared to Australia. A month later Alison rang from Australia to tell Marian that she had aborted her child.'

Alli sucked in a ragged breath. 'Why?'

He shrugged. 'Apparently she was tired of Hugo and thought Marian might want him back. Then, a year or so after that, Marian was informed that she'd been killed in Bangkok. She'd flown into Thailand alone.'

Trying to sort this incredible story out, Alli looked down at her mother's photograph, then glanced at Slade's arrogant, unreadable face. 'So who am I?' she asked in a voice that shook.

'When Marian got your first letter I instigated a search. It's taken this long to find out that her sister lied about the abortion. You are the child she had. And, no, we have no idea why she lied, or why she left you with Hugo a few days after you were born and simply disappeared.'

Alli felt as though she'd taken the first step over a precipice—too late to go back.

As though he sensed her emotions, Slade poured a small amount of brandy into a glass and handed it to her. 'Drink some.'

She obeyed, shuddering as the liquid burned down her throat. It did help, though; when the alcohol hit her empty stomach, warmth eased the chill.

Leaning back against the cushions, Marian said weakly, 'Slade, finish it, please.'

'There's not much left. Hugo Greville changed his

name and took you to Valanu because he'd been at school with the chief and could presume on their friendship to ask for sanctuary.'

Sick at heart, Alli got to her feet and addressed Marian Hawkings for the first time. 'I'm so sorry I brought all this back to you.'

The older woman leaned forward. 'This has been a shock for you too.'

'Not, perhaps, as much as you think. I've always known my mother abandoned me at birth, or very soon afterwards, so nothing much has altered.' She said steadily, 'Thank you for telling me. I'll go now.'

She'd got halfway across the room when Slade joined her. 'I'll take you home,' he said deliberately.

'It's all right—'

'Don't be an idiot.'

She paused, then nodded and went docilely with him, waiting in numb silence while he spoke to Caroline in the hall. Down by the car the sun still caressed the waxen glory of the last camellia flowers, and the harbour scintillated blue and silver, but inside Alli was cold, so cold she thought she'd never get warm again.

Slade said nothing as he drove away, and Alli stared unseeingly ahead, only focusing when the car slowed down outside a sturdy Victorian building.

'Where are we? Why aren't we going back to the Lodge?'

'I live here,' he said, manoeuvring the big vehicle into a parking spot in a basement car park.

She turned a belligerent face to him. 'So? I don't.'

He killed the engine. 'I don't think you should be alone tonight,' he said calmly. 'You're in shock, and

I doubt very much whether you'd care to confide to anyone else what you've heard today, so you might as well stay here.'

'No,' she said dully, struggling to overcome the impact of the appalling story. She couldn't cope with the fact that the woman who'd wreaked such havoc had been her mother.

'Come on,' he said, and leaned over to open her door.

She caught a trace of the subtle scent that was his alone; that purely male scent, she thought confusedly, stamped him as definitely as a scar. 'I don't want to,' she said, a little more strongly.

He sat back and looked at her. 'You'll be perfectly safe,' he said pleasantly enough, although she registered the note of steel through the words.

'Aren't you afraid I might be like my mother?'

He lifted an ironic eyebrow. 'Promiscuous?'

She bit her lip and he said, 'It doesn't matter what you are. I'm not like Marian. I know how to deal with people who annoy me.'

She shivered. 'I need a cup of tea,' she said. 'After that I want to go home.'

'All right.' He hooked an arm into the back and brought out her case. 'You also need a shower to wash the slime off,' he said unexpectedly, and she looked at him in wonder, because that was exactly how she felt—unclean, as though her mother's actions had tainted her from the bones out.

Tiredness overcame her, sapping her courage and determination. She knew she should refuse to go with him, but it was so much easier to allow herself to be carried along on the force of his will.

Without speaking, she walked with Slade across the concrete floor and waited docilely while the lift whisked them upwards.

CHAPTER FIVE

LIKE the man who owned it, Slade's apartment was large and compelling, so close to the harbour that reflected light played over the palette of stone and sand and clay. He showed Alli into a bathroom tiled in marble and left her there after explaining the shower controls.

Taking in its luxury, and the vast glossy leaves of a plant that belonged in some tropical jungle, Alli realised instantly that the room was a purely male domain. No toiletries marred the smooth perfection of the counter, and there was no faint, evocative perfume to hint at a woman's presence.

And she should *not* have felt a swift pang of relief. She stripped and turned on the shower; once in, she bewildered herself by sniffing gingerly at the soap in the shower.

Not even a touch of pine or citrus, so the faint fragrance she noticed whenever she was close to Slade was entirely natural.

'Pheromones,' she muttered. Years ago she'd read an article that suggested people unwittingly used subliminal scent to choose a genetically suitable mate.

If that were so, Slade would produce magnificent babies with her.

Tamping down the hot spurt of sensation somewhere deep in the base of her stomach, she thought stringently, and with Caroline.

70

Probably with every other woman on the planet too. Part of his magnetism was the impact of all that superb male physicality.

Oddly embarrassed, she got out her soap from its container and lathered up.

No wonder Marian Hawkings hadn't wanted to meet her! She must be a living reminder of humiliation and misery. Although logic told her it was ridiculous to take her parents' sins onto herself, she felt smirched. Her emotions were raw, and so painful she had to concentrate on the small things, like rinsing her hair until it squeaked, and wiping out the shower when at last she left it.

When she eventually emerged from the bathroom, every inch of skin scrubbed to just this side of pain, teeth newly cleaned and hair towel-dried, Slade met her at the door.

'I should have told you there's a hairdryer in the cupboard,' he said, examining her with formidable detachment.

Although she tried for polite gratitude, his nearness produced a stilted, ungracious tone. 'Thank you, but if you don't mind my hair wet, I'm fine.' She'd never used one before, and now was not the occasion to try something new.

'Why should I mind? The first time I saw it wet— when you walked out of the lagoon like Venus unveiled—I noticed that it looked like a river of fire,' he said silkily.

Alli's heart jumped. He'd changed too, into a cotton shirt the green of his eyes that moulded his shoulders. His trousers did the same to narrow hips and muscled thighs. Although she now wore her smartest jeans and a camel-coloured jersey that had cost her almost a week's wages, his effortless sophistication made Alli feel she should check for hay in her hair.

The sitting room overlooked the harbour and the long peninsula of the North Shore that ended in the rounded humps of two ancient, tiny volcanoes. Behind loomed the bush-clad triple cone of Rangitoto Island, thrust up from the seabed only a few hundred years ago.

Searching for a neutral topic, Alli commented, 'I'm always surprised when I'm reminded that Auckland is a volcanic field. I wonder when the next explosion will be.'

'I feel as though it happened this afternoon,' he said grimly. 'Come and pour the tea.'

Though he refused a cup.

'I need something a bit stronger.' He added dryly, 'Perhaps I should have asked if you'd like that too?'

'No, thanks.' So far she'd managed to behave with dignity; she wasn't going to jeopardise her control. It was, she thought desperately, about all she had left.

He splashed a small amount of whisky into a glass, half filled it with water, then came to sit opposite her on a huge sofa. She set the teapot down and picked up her cup.

'Put in some sugar,' he said abruptly.

'I don't like—'

'Think of it as medicine.' When she didn't move he leaned over and dropped in a couple of lumps before settling back to survey her through half-closed eyes. 'You're in shock.'

Shock? Oh, yes; when he looked at her like that, a smile curving his hard mouth, his eyes glimmering like jade lit by stars of gold, her throat closed and her heart sped up so much it hammered in her ears. Probably this was what had happened to Victorian maidens when they swooned.

Well, she wasn't going to be ridiculous. She'd seen the sort of woman he liked: sophisticated and elegant. Caroline Forsythe was about as different from her as anyone could be.

She sipped the tea tentatively, making a face at its sweetness, but its comforting heat persuaded her to drink it. Her father had considered coffee only suitable as a way to end dinner.

Glass in hand, Slade leaned back in the leather sofa and surveyed her. 'What do you plan to do now?'

'Do?'

'Do,' he repeated in a pleasant tone, adding with an edge, 'Beyond drinking two cups of tea.'

'Go back to the Lodge,' she said warily. 'Why?'

He was watching her with detached interest, as though she were a rare specimen of insect life. 'It seems strange that someone with a degree in English should be content with a job in the office of a back-packers' lodge frequented mainly by surfers.'

'How did you know—?' She stopped and glared at him. 'Why should I be surprised? You kept tabs on me, didn't you!'

'I always knew exactly what you were doing until you left Valanu,' he said calmly. 'I know you took an extra-mural degree from a New Zealand university and passed with A grades.'

'Was it part of the new manager's job to send you reports on me?' she asked, reining in her anger with an effort that almost chipped her teeth. 'I hope you paid him extra.'

When he spoke his voice was as careless as his shrug. 'I protect my own.'

'It makes my skin crawl to think you've been spying on me,' she retorted passionately.

'I don't take chances. As you can see, Marian is fragile. When I first went to Valanu the only thing I knew about you was that you were Simcox's lover and that you wrote an aggressive letter.'

Outraged, she stared at him. 'I was not his lover! Never!'

'My informant seemed sure of the facts.' He spoke with a calm assurance that made her want to throw the teapot at him. 'And he certainly felt more for you than the care an employer owes to an employee.'

'If you've got a dirty mind and listen to stupid gossip it might have seemed like that,' she returned with relish. 'That doesn't mean it was the truth.'

His ironic smile hid whatever he was thinking. 'It doesn't matter now.'

Alli wanted it to matter. She wanted, she discovered with something very close to horror, him to be furiously jealous. Alarmed, she steered the subject in a different direction. 'Given your opinion, what made you change your mind about contacting me?'

'Facts,' he said laconically.

When she directed a blank look at him he elaborated, 'Once I realised you looked like Marian's sister I got one of my information people to find the truth. It took her a while, for various reasons.'

'The name change?'

He nodded. 'Alison told everyone that she and

Hugo were going back to Britain. Quite a lot of time was wasted trying to track them down there. The logical thing for them to have done was cross the Tasman Sea—in those days you didn't need passports to travel between Australia and New Zealand. It took a while for the researcher to find them.'

'Do you think my—Alison tried to put them off the scent?' She held her breath while he drank a little of the whisky.

'It seems a logical assumption. Then, of course, your father changed his name and yours when he went to Valanu, but eventually we pieced together a sequence of events, backed by legal documents. The records proved you were Marian's niece. But by then you'd left Valanu.'

'I'm surprised you bothered looking,' she snapped.

'Ah, there's a difference between an opportunist and a relative.' His mouth twisted in a smile that held equal amounts of wryness and mockery. 'Then the television news shortened the search by showing you hauling shipwrecked yachtsmen through the surf.'

'And you recognised me?' she said, before she could stop the words.

'I never forget a good pair of legs.' His smile was hard and cynical.

He was baiting her. Ignoring it, she said, 'Why did Marian decide to see me? Unless she wants to prove once and for all that I'm not her daughter. She doesn't have to—I won't insist on a DNA test. The photograph and my birth certificate are proof enough for me.'

When Slade didn't answer, she looked up and saw that he was swirling the liquid in his glass with an expression she couldn't interpret. Eyes enigmatic, he parried her enquiring gaze.

Something in her heart tightened unbearably. She said with stiff pride, 'If she wants to establish once and for all that I have no claim on her I'm perfectly willing to sign a disclaimer.'

His dark lashes came down to hide his eyes. In a level voice he said, 'It's not so easy. In certain cases signing a disclaimer might not be enough. New Zealand law can be tricky.'

Which meant that he, at least, had considered and researched the options. Alli swallowed more of the tea, shuddering at its cloying sweetness. 'So why did she want to see me?'

'I suspect that she felt you deserved to know your own parentage.'

'That's—kind of her,' she said reluctantly.

'And perhaps because you are her only living relative.'

Alli pointed out, 'She's got you.'

Slade watched her covertly as he drank some of the whisky and set his glass down on the table. 'But there's no blood relationship.'

Some years after his own mother had died Marian had come into his life like summer, bringing laughter and life and love into a silent, grieving house. That childhood adoration had matured into a protective love that still held.

'In Valanu,' Alli said quietly, 'a child can live with another family and he'll consider everyone in both his birth family and his adoptive family to be his kin.'

'In New Zealand the same thing happens amongst

Maori families. But Marian grew up in England,' he said briefly, 'and things are different there.'

When she said brusquely, 'I know that,' he examined her tantalising face from beneath his lashes, wondering about her life on the island.

'Were you fostered by another family?'

'No.' She tempered her abrupt reply by adding more mildly, 'I did spend a lot of time with the family next door.'

'Ah, the home of the lovelorn Tama,' he observed blandly.

He was almost sorry when Alli ignored the taunt. 'I don't think you can be right about Marian; after all, she must have hated my—my mother. Why would she want anything to do with me?'

He shrugged. 'You know why—she now has the information she needs to convince her that you are her niece. You have a certain look of her father, apparently.'

This clearly didn't satisfy her, but it was all he was going to tell her. He watched her pick up her teacup again, her lovely face absorbed, the exquisite curve of her cheekbones stirring something feral into smouldering life inside him.

When he saw tears gather on her lashes he was astonished at the swift knot of tension in his groin. Even when she was distressed and unsure of herself, her glowing golden sensuousness reached out and grabbed him, angering him with an awareness of his vulnerability. He had to exert all his will not to pick her up and let her cry out her disillusionment and pain on his shoulder.

Any excuse to get her in your arms again, he

thought savagely, despising himself. After two years he should have been able to kill this mindless, degrading lust. His lovers were chosen for more than their sexuality; it infuriated him that this woman's face and body had lodged in his brain for years, stripping away his prized control.

Deliberately, he sat back and decided to let her cry. She'd been unnaturally composed after listening to the real story of her life; weeping would help ease her shock.

'Sorry,' she muttered, getting to her feet and striding to the window with less than her usual grace.

Slade found himself following her. This, he thought grimly as he walked across to stand behind her, must have been how her father had felt—helpless in the face of an overwhelming hunger.

He, however, wouldn't allow himself to be dazzled by a face and a seductive body.

Or the unusual urge to protect her. His lovers were independent women, more than capable of looking after themselves. Nothing he'd seen or heard of Alli Pierce made him think she was any different, and too much hung on her character for him to lower his guard.

She was staring out of the window; when he came up behind her, her shoulders went rigid, but she didn't move. Gently he turned her around.

'It will probably leave you with a headache,' he said, gut-punched by the tears spilling from her great lion-gold eyes onto the tragic mask of her face, 'but I've read somewhere that crying is the best way to deal with stress.'

She gulped. 'Screaming and th-throwing a

t-tantrum is a lot more positive,' she muttered, and suddenly her defences were breached and she began to cry, great silent sobs that tore through her slender body.

In a way she had been alone all her life, but she had never before been faced with her utter isolation; when her father had died she'd had friends, the time-honoured rituals of island life to console her.

Marian Hawkings might be her aunt, but she wanted nothing to do with her, and who could blame her? The mother she'd fantasised about and the father she'd never really known had taken the secrets of their guilty love to the grave.

But even as she shivered she was enfolded in warmth. Slade Hawkings pulled her against his big body and held her while she wept into his shoulder, his cheek on the top of her head, his heart thudding into hers.

He even thrust a handkerchief into her hand as though she were a lost child; the simple gesture made her cry even more.

Eventually the sobs subsided into hiccups, and she blew her nose and stepped back, wiping her eyes so that he couldn't see how embarrassed she was.

'Feeling better?' he asked, his deep voice so detached she knew he was wondering how to get rid of her.

'Not at the moment,' she mumbled. 'But at least I haven't got a full-blown headache.'

'Go and wash your face and I'll pour you a brandy,' he said.

'I don't need one, thanks.' She fled into the bathroom and stared, horrified, at her face, puffy and mottled and tear-stained.

Cold water ruthlessly splashed on helped, and so did a brisk mental talking-to, and the swift application of lipstick.

But it took every shred of will-power she possessed to close the door behind her and walk into that elegant sitting room with her head held high and her chin angled just the right side of defiance.

'Brandy,' Slade said with an enigmatic smile, handing her a large glass with a minuscule amount of liquid in it. 'Drink it down and then I think we should go for a walk.'

She stared at him as though he was crazy. 'A walk? Here?'

'There are places.' When she didn't move he said more gently, 'I know you don't like it, but it does help.'

So he'd noticed her involuntary grimace at Marian's apartment. The taste hadn't improved, but it must have had some effect on her because after she'd drained it she said, 'All right, let's go for a walk.'

He parked the car at the foot of one of the little volcanic cones that dotted the isthmus. Silently they walked up the steep side, terraced by sheep tracks as well as trenches built centuries ago to defend the huge fort that had been the local Maoris refuge against enemies.

Although she considered herself fit, by halfway Alli was puffing, her mind fixed on one thing only—getting there. Pride forbade her to suggest a few moments' rest.

Slade's long, powerful legs covered the ground

with ease, and when they reached the top he stood with the wind teasing his black hair and glanced at her searchingly.

She knew what she looked like—red-faced and gasping. Yet one green look from him made adrenalin pump through her, banishing tiredness in a flash of acute awareness. When he smiled, she was mesmerised.

'Auckland,' he said, and gestured around them.

What's happening to me? she thought, unbearably stimulated. Instinct gave her the answer: you're attracted to him.

No, she thought feverishly. *Attracted* is not the way to describe this overwhelming response.

Struggling to reclaim some scraps of poise, she stared at the panorama below them—a leafy city between two harbours, the dark lines of hills forming other boundaries, islands in a sea turned pink by the light of the setting sun.

It's quite simple and uncomplicated, she thought despairingly. You want Slade desperately and dangerously, on some hidden, primeval level you didn't even know existed until you met him.

It terrified her, this hot, sweet flood of desire, as limitless as the ocean, as fierce as a cyclone in the wide Pacific, as tempting as a mango on a hot day...

And hard on that discovery came another. Was this what had driven her parents to betray Marian?

'Alison—'

'Don't call me that,' she said, shuddering. 'Grown up or not, I've decided I prefer Alli.'

'I can't say I blame you,' he said unexpectedly.

'If it's the truth—'

'It is.' He spoke with such utter conviction that she believed him. 'I've never heard Marian tell a lie.'

'So my parents were sleazes of the highest degree. I don't want to be linked with them, not even by name.'

'Sometimes the truth has many facets. Your father was hugely respected in Valanu.'

Unsurprised that he knew this, she nodded. Ian Pierce had organised the accounts for the tribal corporation, helping them deal with trade and bureaucracy.

Slade resumed, 'You can't deny the link, no matter how much you disapprove of what they did. You set this process in motion. All right, so you've found out a few facts that you don't like, but they were your parents. I have no idea what your mother was like, but part of her is in you. And I presume you loved your father?'

Eyes filled with the glowing pink-mauve sky over a distant range of hills, Alli said, 'I don't know. I suppose I took him for granted. He didn't neglect me—he was firm and he made sure I ate properly and that I knew right from wrong.'

But he'd never cuddled her, or told her he loved her, or kissed her; although parcels of books had arrived several times a year he'd never read a bedtime story to her. When she'd been happy or sad or hurt she'd taken herself to Tama's family along the road. From them she'd learned about love and laughter and how to quarrel—all the subtle intricacies of relationships.

'He wouldn't be the first man to love not wisely

but too well.' A cynical inflection coloured Slade's comment.

'If it *was* love.'

'If it wasn't, he certainly wouldn't be the first man to lust unwisely and too much.' A note of derision ran through his voice.

But not you, she thought, humiliated afresh. Slade wouldn't think the world well lost for passion. He had too much self-control.

'Now that you know the circumstances of your birth,' he said, 'do you intend to take this further? Do you want to track down your father's family?'

She shuddered inwardly. 'Right now, no. I feel dreadful for bringing it all back to Marian—and I feel tainted.'

'An over-reaction. Of them all, you were the innocent one.'

'Marian and me,' she said, thinking that although his pragmatism was as sharply aggressive as a cold bucket of water in the face, it was also oddly comforting.

'As I pointed out before, you have only Marian's side of the story. Your mother might have had another one. If their behaviour disgusts you, make sure you don't follow their example.'

Was he referring to her supposed affair with Barry Simcox? She gave a sardonic smile. 'That's easy enough. As far as I know I have no sisters to betray.'

A car drove up to the parking area and disgorged a group of boisterous, laughing adolescents who swarmed up to the obelisk with much yelled banter. Someone produced a camera; Alli flinched at the flash, envying them their noisy, cheerful ease.

'You know what I mean.' Slade watched the young people with an alertness that reminded her of a warrior. 'If anything about your behaviour worries you, fight it. There is nothing will-power can't overcome.'

Probably the tenet he lived by! She blinked when the sun dipped behind the hills. 'It'll be dark soon— shouldn't we be heading back down?'

'We'll walk down the road.' He took her elbow and urged her onto the sealed surface. 'It's well lit.'

Keeping her eyes rigidly on the black bitumen ahead, she pulled away from him. He dropped her arm, but strode beside her.

Of all the shocks this day had brought, the knowledge that from tomorrow she'd never see him again was the one that hurt the most.

Surreptitiously she straightened her shoulders. When she'd first fought his disturbing, dangerous charisma, she'd been able to overwhelm it with constructive and vigorous resentment because he'd forced her to stay on Valanu.

Unfortunately, this time he'd been aloofly kind. Dislike and outrage weren't going to rescue her; she'd have to fall back on will-power.

So he was gorgeous? So he made her stomach quiver and her bones melt and turned her brain to soup? Get over it, she told herself with tough common sense. After all, she'd been totally unmoved by other gorgeous men.

But none of them had had Slade's combination of compelling physical appeal and inherent strength and authority.

And then there was Caroline Forsythe, who was probably in love with him.

Night fell softly around them, and the lights of the city shone out to combat the increasing depth of darkness.

Slade didn't give anything away, but his beloved stepmother's goddaughter had to be a better partner for him than a woman who'd be a constant reminder to Marian Hawkings of shame and treachery.

A better partner? Listen to yourself, she thought with harsh scorn; what sort of fantasy are you spinning? Stop being so stupidly, wilfully, madly ridiculous.

Slade neither trusted nor liked her, and, although his potent sexuality made her too aware of her own femininity, she didn't know what she really thought of him.

Yells from behind and the sound of car doors slamming amidst gales of laughter swivelled her head around.

'Stay well on the side,' Slade commanded.

At the first squeal of brakes he swore beneath his breath and pushed her across the road onto the downward side, locking her against him as he dived over the edge into the darkness.

He twisted so that he landed beneath her, his hard body cushioning her fall. Gasping, she lay sprawled across him, wincing as a harsh, grating noise from the other side of the road was followed by a heavy thump and the sound of metal crumpling and tearing.

'Are you all right?' Slade demanded fiercely, his arms tightening around her.

'Yes,' she croaked. 'Are you?'

'I'm fine.' Apparently not convinced by her answer, he ran his hands over her arms and down her legs. Only then did he push her into a sitting position and say, 'Do you know anything about first aid?'

Alli scrambled to her feet, heart chilling as a scream sawed through the mild air. 'I've done a course,' she said, trying to remember one thing—any-thing—she'd learned. 'Check the breathing first,' she said aloud.

'OK.' He hauled her up the steep grassy bank and onto the road, where he thrust a mobile phone into her hands. 'Ring 111 and then SND. When they ask what service you want, tell them it's an accident on the Summit Road on One Tree Hill.'

'Be careful,' she blurted when he turned away. 'The car might explode.'

He gave her an odd glance and said ironically, 'And people might die. Don't worry—it's not on fire.'

He disappeared over the far edge of the road as Alli fumbled with the numbers before following him.

A few seconds later she told the woman who answered, 'At least five are hurt—one's on her feet, helping get the driver out, and one's sitting on the grass. She looks as though she's broken her arm. One's screaming, but she doesn't seem badly hurt.'

'And the others?'

'Two have been thrown out—they don't seem to be moving.'

'All right, we'll get ambulances there as soon as we can,' the woman said calmly. 'Check those on the ground—airways first, then breathing, then circula-tion. If they're a safe distance from the car don't move them.'

Alli went to each in turn, hugely relieved to dis-cover that both men were breathing regularly. One had blood on his face, but when she touched his cheek he opened his eyes and frowned at her. The other didn't move.

She stood up, intending to head for the girl with the broken arm, when the one who'd been screaming came rushing across and tried to fling herself onto the unconscious man.

'No!'

Alli managed to stop her, but the girl turned on her, lashing out and sobbing, 'He's dead. I know he's dead!'

Slade grabbed her and pinned her arms, commanding harshly, 'Stop that, or I'll slap you.'

For a second she stared into his face, until his ruthless determination cut through her shock. Blinking, choking on her tears, she whimpered, 'He's dead.'

'He's not dead,' Slade told her.

The sound of a siren wailed up from below. 'OK, that's the ambulance,' Slade said. Releasing the girl, he said to the one who'd helped him assess the driver, 'Take her round the next corner and wave it down.'

'Come on, Lissa.' Her friend touched the girl's arm and together they walked down the road.

Slade asked, 'How are the others?'

'One is conscious; he's breathing freely.' She indicated the girl with the broken arm. 'I haven't had a chance to see how she is.'

She was white and in pain, but she said, 'I'm all right. They made us girls put the seat belts on. And Simon had one too, of course.' She bit her lip and looked across at the car. 'He's the driver. Is he all right?'

'He seems to be.'

'What about the others? H-how are they?'

Alli said quietly, 'They're breathing, and they look pretty good to me. I'm sorry, but I won't touch your arm—I think it's best to wait for the ambulance staff to deal with it.'

An hour later, after they'd both given their accounts of the accident to an efficient young constable and been given a lift down the hill, Slade slid behind the wheel of his car and said briefly, 'Come on, let's go home.'

'Home?' Alli said on a slight quaver.

'I'm not taking you back to the Lodge now,' he said brusquely, backing the car out of the parking space. 'I've got a spare bedroom—you can spend the night there.'

When she opened her mouth to protest, he cut in, 'You'll be quite safe.'

'What about Caroline?'

Slade looked left and right, then eased out into the stream of traffic. 'What,' he said pleasantly, 'about her?'

The words like bricks in her mouth, Alli said, 'I thought she might have some reason to mind.'

'No reason,' he said.

Silently they drove beneath the streetlights until they reached his apartment.

CHAPTER SIX

SLADE'S spare bedroom intimidated Alli with its excellent taste.

He smiled ironically at her quick glance around, and said, 'Spare rooms do have a tendency to look like hotel rooms. A quilt from Valanu would make it more exciting.'

Dangerously cheered because he'd remembered such a minor thing, she said, 'But much less elegant. The decorator would have a fit. Anyway, I think it suits you.'

She flushed when he eyed her with an amused gleam in his green eyes. 'I'm not sure how to take that,' he observed. 'Cold and unwelcoming?'

'Restrained,' she said firmly.

The amusement vanished from his gaze, leaving it unreadable. 'The bathroom is through that door over there. Do you need anything?'

'No, thank you.' What had she said to be so completely rebuffed?

Up until then he'd been the perfect host; he'd persuaded her to eat, and been concerned when she'd only been able to manage two slices of toast. Because the edge of challenge in his tone had muted she'd let herself relax.

Now it was like standing next to a glacier.

Thick lashes veiling his gaze, Slade nodded. 'In that case, goodnight, Alli.'

After he'd left the room she showered, startled to discover blood on her skin and clothes. One of the men who'd been thrown from the car was in a dangerous coma; another, with the casual beneficence of fate, had suffered nothing more than mild concussion and a cut arm. The driver apparently would be all right too.

Once in bed, she felt her thoughts buzz around her mind in wild confusion; the adrenalin crash made sleep seem an unattainable nirvana. She listened to the alien sounds of the city, trying to block out the wail of a distant siren with the remembered roar of waves pounding the reef in Valanu.

Restlessly she turned on her back and stared at the ceiling, trying to push an unwelcome truth away. Valanu was her past; she couldn't go back. Besides, she wanted to be here—just through the wall from Slade…

When the dream began she recognised it, but as always, although she knew what was coming, she couldn't snap free from the prison of her mind.

She was cold, so cold the ice in her veins crackled when she moved. It stabbed her mercilessly with a thousand tiny knives, yet she had to keep going, had to find a warm place before the ice reached her heart. Panting, mindlessly terrified, she forced herself to run through the empty, echoing corridors of an immense house, hammering on every door she came to. Most of the rooms were empty, but occasionally she'd come to one and see light through the keyhole, hear laughing voices.

Then she'd call out, but entry was always refused, even after she begged to be allowed in. All she wanted was a few seconds in front of the fires she could hear crackling behind each obdurate door.

Eventually, all tears frozen, she found herself out in a bleak forest, with snow falling in soft drifts. She forced herself on until the drifts caught her feet and she fell. Shivering, she had to crawl...

But this time she didn't feel the terrifying ice creep through her veins. This time someone came and picked her up and carried her into the warmth. And when at last sleep claimed her she was in sheltering arms that melted the snow and kept the howling winds at bay...

She woke to heat, the gold of sunlight through her eyelids, and a subtle, teasing scent...

Lashes flying up, Alli jerked sideways, body pumping with adrenalin. Beside her Slade stirred, muscles flexing under far too much sleek bronze skin. He didn't appear to be wearing any clothes.

'Stop wriggling,' he murmured, his voice rich and slightly slurred.

When she gasped he woke instantly, without moving. Recognition narrowed his eyes into metallic green shards. Obeying instinct, Alli jack-knifed out of the bed.

Slade rolled over to link his hands behind his head and survey her with formidable self-possession. Alli suffered it a second before realising that while her T-shirt covered the essentials the briefs she wore beneath it revealed every inch of her long legs—inches he was now assessing with a heavy-lidded gaze and a hard smile.

She didn't have the self-assurance to walk away from him looking like some good-time girl from a men's magazine, but neither was she going to reveal her embarrassment by scuttling across to her clothes.

Abruptly she sat down on the edge of the bed, as far away from him as she could, and hauled the sheet over her legs. His dark brows rose.

Alli swallowed, but her parched throat made the words gritty and indistinct. 'What the hell is going on?'

'Perhaps you could tell me that?' he suggested, subtle menace running through the words like silk.

She wanted desperately to lick her dry lips, but something stopped her. Instead she demanded childishly, 'What are you doing in my bed?'

'Before you start accusing me of rape—'

Her blood ran cold. 'Rape?' she croaked.

'Relax. Nothing happened.' The flinty speculation in his eyes belied his mocking tone. 'Unless crawling down the hall making pathetic whimpering noises could be called an event.'

Humiliation flooded through her. *'What?'*

He stretched and sat up, exposing far more skin than she could deal with. 'You appear to be a sleep-walker.'

Vague scraps of the dream swirled around her. She shut her eyes against both it and the effect his sleek bronze chest was having on her already strained nerves. 'Oh, God. What did I do?'

'You huddled dramatically on all fours outside my door, muttering that you were frozen, that you had to get close to the fire before the snow killed you.'

Rigid with mortification, she said, 'I—I haven't had that dream for years. And I haven't walked in my sleep since I was a kid. I'm sorry I inflicted it on you.'

'I imagine yesterday was traumatic enough to wake any number of old devils,' he said objectively.

Something struck her, and she opened her eyes to glare at him, trying to ignore the way the mellow light through the curtains burnished his broad shoulders and tangled in the male pattern of hair across his chest. He was utterly breathtaking in his potent male confidence. 'But—why are you here?'

'I carried you back, put you between the sheets and endeavoured to leave. You had other ideas,' he told her, the laconic irony in his tone lacerating her pride even more. 'Besides, your feet and hands were frozen. I planned to wait until you were warmed up and safely asleep, but every time I started to get out you woke crying and pleading, and in the end staying here seemed the easiest solution.'

Shamed colour swept across her face, then drained away. 'You could have woken me up,' she said lamely.

He shrugged, muscles coiled beneath his skin. Hastily Alli looked down at the floor, using every ounce of energy to resist the hot, untamed need that roared into life in the pit of her stomach.

Slade told her, 'I tried that too, but you didn't respond. Not even when I called your name.'

Desperately she said, 'I'm sorry.'

'Don't worry about it.'

There was no sophisticated way she could get out of this. Closing her eyes a second, she said, 'I—well, thank you.'

'At least we both got some sleep,' he said dryly.

'And now, if you don't mind, I'll leave you.' When she stared at him, he added in a tone that could have dried up a large river, 'I normally sleep naked, but I did have the sense to drag on a pair of briefs. If it doesn't embarrass you...' He started to fling back the covers.

Alli clamped her eyes shut and sat stiffly, longing for him to go and leave her to collapse into a puddle of raw chagrin.

He'd reached the door when she heard him drawl, 'I hope I don't have to tell you that if this was a ploy it didn't work.'

Her eyes flew open. Like some bronze god, from the arrogant carriage of his head to the set of his wide shoulders, he hadn't turned fully to face her, so the twist of his spine outlined the pattern and swell of muscles across his back.

Never before, she thought dazedly, had she appreciated the male triangle of wide shoulders and narrow hips, barely concealed by briefs. Sensation scorching through her, she dragged her gaze away from the long, powerful legs.

'A ploy?' she snarled. 'You must be joking.'

One black brow lifted. 'I've never been more serious. I don't let anyone blackmail me, and I don't fight fair.'

His level words sent a chill through her. Keeping her gaze level and composed, she retorted, 'So it's just as well I don't want to fight and I'm not a blackmailer.'

Her stomach churned when he gave her an edged smile and walked out, closing the door firmly behind him and leaving behind an impression of streamlined strength and ruthless, formidable power.

And a compelling male sexuality so potent Alli's pulse was still racing half an hour later, when she emerged from her bedroom, showered and dressed in the clothes she'd worn to see Marian Hawkings.

Following distant sounds, she arrived at the kitchen, where Slade was dealing efficiently with an impressive espresso machine.

'What do you want done with the sheets and towels?' she asked, hoping that the curtness of her voice concealed the jolt of arousal spiking through her.

'Leave them.'

'I've stripped the bed.'

He pushed a cup of black coffee towards her. 'Leave them, Alli. I have a housekeeper who'll deal with them.'

'Lucky you,' she said, and turned on her heel.

'Alli?'

She kept going.

'Don't put me to the bother of coming after you,' he said, his cool words underpinned by inflexible determination. 'You may not have had a mother, but from the little I've heard about your father he'd have made sure you were taught manners.'

'And I'm sure you know it's not polite to order around your guests—however unwelcome, seedy and suspect—as though they were your servants,' she returned.

His wry laugh shocked her.

'Touché,' he said. 'Except that I should point out that good servants are far too rare nowadays to treat badly. Come and have some breakfast. Tui told me you're pretty impossible in the morning until you've eaten.'

Alli turned slowly. 'Nonsense. I just don't like being accused—'

'I can't remember accusing you of anything,' he stated grimly. 'Especially of being seedy and suspect.' He paused, then added, 'Or unwelcome.'

Slade watched her glorious eyes darken into mystery. She said, 'I *know* I'm unwelcome, and you implied the rest when you told me you didn't blackmail easily.'

She was an enigma. Last night a weeping bundle of terror, this morning incandescent with indignation until he mentioned her sleepwalking—if that was what it was.

Courted since he'd grown into his shoulders in his mid-teens, experience had taught Slade that he could act like an ancient despot and some women would still pursue him.

Money, he thought cynically as Alli hovered in the doorway, talked very loudly.

'You are not unwelcome,' he said curtly. 'I'm sorry if I made you feel that you were. Do you want this coffee or not?'

'It certainly sounded as though you thought that— that I'd tried to set you up,' she said, but she came back warily into the kitchen.

She lifted the mug to her mouth, hiding behind it, but when she drank her lips moved in a slight, sensuous movement that made him glad he had a counter between them.

Last night had been endless. He'd lain in her bed in the darkness, so aroused by her soft curves and satiny skin that it had taken all his control to leash his hunger. It served him right for telling her so pompously that will-power could do anything!

Even now he desired her with a desperation that came too close to clouding his brain. In spite of the promptings of caution he wanted to believe it had been a nightmare that had driven her in search of some human warmth during the night. Although she'd clung to him she'd made no overt indication of wanting sex, seeming content to snuggle in his arms like a bird sheltering from a storm.

But he'd learned in a hard school not to take things at face value, and lust guaranteed poor decisions. He didn't know enough about Alli to risk trusting her.

Too much depended on not screwing up—and that, he thought, clamping down on memories of her body against him in bed, was not the most felicitous word to use!

'Tell me about the dream.' He poured himself a cup of coffee.

She hesitated, then shrugged. 'It's always the same—one of those self-repeating sagas. I'm looking for shelter, but no one will let me in.'

'Orphan in the storm? You kept muttering about being cold.' He watched as she took another mouthful of the hot liquid, noting the catspaws rippling its surface. Her hand was trembling.

'Yes—well, that's part of it. I know that if I don't get warm I'll die.'

She hadn't been shivering when he'd found her outside his door. In fact she'd been locked in stasis, her body rigid, not even moving when he'd searched for the pulse in her throat.

He could still feel the silken skin beneath his fingertips.

Ruthlessly he forced his mind back to the straighter path of logic. Her hands and feet, however, had been cold. 'No wonder you were terrified.'

Her shoulders lifted a fraction and she drank some more coffee, holding the mug as though she still needed to warm her hands. 'Children often have that sort of recurring dream, but mostly they grow out of it.'

'I'm surprised you dream of the cold when you couldn't have ever experienced it on Valanu.'

She stared at him for a time, golden-brown eyes thoughtful. 'Until now I've never thought of that. Interesting, isn't it?' she finally said. 'Although I had *Grimms' Fairy Tales*, so I knew there was such a thing.'

The peal of a doorbell made her jump; when she looked suspiciously at him he said, 'I'll be back in a minute.'

Alli watched him go, her taut nerves wound even more tightly. Who could this be—friends? A quick glance at her watch dispelled that idea; only very intimate friends would turn up before eight in the morning. Caroline Forsythe?

The opening of the kitchen door brought her upright, her armour tightly fastened around her.

'Breakfast,' Slade said, carrying a couple of takeaway packages. 'Bring your coffee and we'll eat it in the next room.'

She followed him into a combination dining and living room, less formal than the room she'd seen yesterday. Comfortable and expansive, it channelled the morning sun through a wall of glass doors. Outside, lounging furniture looked over the water from a wide, long terrace.

Slade unloaded the boxes onto a table and proceeded to set out the food. Noting her swift glance at the harbour, decorated with its colourful weekend bunting of sails, he said, 'It's still chilly outside—too cold to eat there in comfort.'

'I'm getting acclimatised to New Zealand's climate.' She gave a soft laugh. 'At first I thought I'd never get warm again.'

'Cereal?' he asked.

Another hungry growl from her stomach reminded her she'd had no dinner the previous night. 'Yes, please,' she said simply.

Incredibly, sharing the first meal of the day with him brought a wary happiness. As she ate her cereal, and the splendid Eggs Benedict that he'd unpacked, they discussed Valanu and the resort, and the people Slade had dealt with there.

'How is the chief?' he asked idly.

She swallowed the last of the delectable eggs and smiled. 'Very well. He's talking about a joint fishing venture with the Sant'Rosans.'

'And his son? Second son,' he amended blandly.

'Tama? He's fine,' she said stiffly. 'He's doing an administrative degree here in Auckland, and otherwise he spends a lot of his time, I'm told, nagging his father and the tribal council for more and more money for health issues.'

Slade's black brows quirked. 'Is he married?'

'Yes, to a charming Auckland girl.'

'Did you mind?'

'Not in the least.' She smiled with sunny nonchalance. 'His father has finally forgiven him, and the last photo Sisilu sent me was of the chief at a meeting with a small blonde girl perched on his knee.'

'And Barry Simcox?' When she looked blank he said lazily, 'I assumed you'd keep in touch?'

'No. Isn't he working for you now?'

'Not for a couple of years.' He offered her a bowl of fresh fruit. 'Try the cherimoya—it's like eating tangy custard. How about the dragon lady who ran the dancing troupe?'

Alli laughed. 'She's fine too. Still terrifying the manager into doing whatever she wants him to.'

He was, she thought after breakfast, when she went to get her bag, a good companion. His keen mind stimulated her, like his somewhat cynical sense of humour, and to her surprise she'd discovered that they shared some favourite writers and singers.

When he wanted to be he was utterly charming, but his charm masked a dangerously compelling strength. Skin tightening, she tried to banish the memory of waking up next to him. Had his hand been curved around her waist, or had that been another dream?

A nice one this time…

'He was asleep until you did your outraged virgin bit. He probably thought you were one of his girlfriends,' she said severely to her reflection, and carried her pack out into the hall.

He was waiting by the front door, but as she came towards him the telephone rang. 'Excuse me,' he said without hurry. 'I'll take it in the office.'

Alli lowered her pack to the floor and examined a

magnificent, almost abstract landscape that was definitely New Zealand. It was a bush scene, sombre yet vibrant. With a myriad of greens and browns the artist had conveyed the sense of peril and hidden mystery she'd noticed in the New Zealand forest.

She thought nostalgically of the waters of the lagoon at Valanu—every shade of blue melding into glowing turquoise beneath a brilliant sky. Sometimes she dreamed of the soft hush of trade winds in the coconut palms, and the crunch of blazing white sand beneath her feet.

Safer than dreaming about snow, she thought sardonically.

Yet she was learning to love New Zealand. The parts of it she'd seen were beautiful in a wild, aloof way.

On a table beneath the bush picture a nude bronze art deco dancer postured with sinuous abandon. Absorbed in its mannered, erotic grace, Alli jumped when Slade spoke from behind her.

'That was Marian.'

Composing her face so that he wouldn't read the sudden wild hope there, she turned around slowly. 'Oh?'

'She wants to see you before I take you home,' he said briefly. 'It won't be much of a delay.'

Alli could read nothing in his face. 'Did she say why?'

'No.' He opened the front door, holding it to let her through in front of him.

They drove along Auckland's streets, busy with tourists and those who'd decided to eat brunch beside the harbour on this sunny Sunday morning.

Alli tried to rein in her seething thoughts, glad when Slade said abruptly, 'I rang the hospital this morning to find out how those kids were.'

'I meant to ask you at breakfast,' she said remorsefully. It had fled her mind because she'd been enjoying herself so much.

'They've all been discharged except the boy in the coma and the girl with the broken arm. She'll be discharged this morning, and the boy is critical but stable.'

'I do hope he recovers without any damage. The boys insisted that the girls wear the seat belts,' she said. 'They were so boisterous I wondered if they'd been drinking, but it didn't seem as though they had.'

'High on youth,' he commented dispassionately.

Alli glanced at him, her stomach tightening at the arrogant symmetry of line and angle that was his profile. How did he do it? she thought desperately. Being with him sharpened all her senses; today the sky was brighter, the perfume of jasmine through the window more musky and evocative, the texture of her clothes against her skin supple and fine and erotically charged.

Once more they took the silent lift up to the fourth floor. This time it was Marian who opened the door—a Marian much more composed than on the previous day. She accepted Slade's kiss, and then asked Alli, 'My dear, how did you sleep?'

'Fine, thank you,' Alli said mundanely, relaxing only when their hostess waved them into the room where she'd received them the previous day.

'Do sit down,' she said, and settled into her chair, examining Alli with a small frown between her exquisitely plucked brows. 'I was shocked when Caroline told me that Slade had rung to say you'd had to deal with an accident—what a ghastly thing! I'd have nightmares for a week!'

Without looking at Slade, Alli replied, 'At least only one person was badly hurt.'

'Do you know how he is?'

Concisely Slade explained what he'd learned.

Marian sighed. 'I feel for his poor parents.'

A slight pause stretched Alli's nerves to breaking point. She felt completely alien in this luxurious room—and that was odd, because she hadn't felt like that in Slade's apartment.

Marian picked up an envelope from the table beside her chair and held it out. 'I asked you here this morning because I want to give you something.'

Alli tensed. If she's offering me money, she thought disjointedly, I'll—I'll throw it at her!

Fingers trembling, she opened it. But there was no money. Intensely relieved, she took out a photograph and examined it, her heart contracting; this time the woman was in full face, eyeing the camera with a half-smile. In colouring and features she was almost identical to the face Alli saw in her mirror every morning.

She looked across at the older woman.

'Yes,' Marian said, 'it's your mother.'

Blindly, Alli turned it over. Her mother's handwriting was a bold scrawl. *To my sister Marian,* she'd written. *So you don't forget me.*

Well, running away with her sister's husband had made sure of that!

'Thank you.' Then she suddenly remembered

something, and scrabbled in her bag until she found an envelope. 'I don't know whether you want this, but it's a—it's yours, anyway.'

She held it out. Automatically Marian accepted it, but she didn't open it. 'What is it?'

'It's a wedding photograph I found in my father's things,' Alli said uncomfortably.

Another awkward pause followed, broken by Marian's quick reply. 'No, I don't want it, I'm afraid.' She handed it back. 'Do you know anything about your mother at all?'

Alli tucked the photograph of her mother into the envelope and put it in her bag. 'Nothing. My father never spoke of her.'

For a moment the older woman looked inexpressibly sad, but the fleeting expression vanished under the mask of a good hostess. 'Were you happy as a child?'

Alli gave her a brilliant smile and stood up, Slade following suit. 'In lots of ways I had a super childhood. Children are very resilient, you know. They accept things.'

Marian's glance tangled with Slade's. 'Yes, I know. I'm glad you were happy.' She got to her feet and led the way to the door.

But before they reached it she stopped and turned to Alli. 'Thank you for coming to see me,' she said unexpectedly. 'You must have felt like telling me to go to hell when I rejected your approach so comprehensively two years ago. But your existence came as a...' she hesitated, as though discarding the word that came naturally to her tongue and substituting another

'...a huge shock. I thought you'd—never been born, you see.'

It was, Alli could see, all the excuse she was going to give. And it was also a definite goodbye. She didn't blame the older woman; each sight of her niece had to be an exercise in remembered bitterness.

'It's all right,' she said swiftly. 'I do understand. Thank you for giving me this photograph—I'll treasure it.'

Marian's smile was a mere sketch, and before she could speak Slade said, 'It's time we went, Alli.'

'Caroline will be so sorry to have missed you,' Marian said.

But Caroline must have come in while they were talking, because she was in the hall when they came out. Alli felt the other woman's resentment, cloaked though it was with a gracious smile, when Caroline asked, 'Are you going to be at the Thorpes' tonight, Slade?'

'Yes,' he said, smiling at her.

'Oh, good. I'll see you there, then.' Her look at Alli held a flicker of smugness. 'Lovely to have met you, Alison. Goodbye.'

Less subtle than Marian's farewell, but no less definite. Alli nodded and said goodbye, and went out with Slade into a blue and gold and crystal day, warm as a welcome and heady as champagne.

Its beauty was almost wasted. As they drove north they spoke little. A few hours ago she'd woken up in this man's arms; by the time they reached the Lodge she felt as though he'd withdrawn to the other side of the moon.

Sadness almost closed her throat.

'Who was it,' Slade remarked as they swung off the road onto the rutted track that led to the Lodge, 'that said to be careful what you wish for because you might get it?'

'Bluebeard, probably,' Alli returned jauntily. 'Don't worry, I'm not shattered. I was surprised to discover that my upright father was an adulterer—and with his wife's sister—but I suppose I always suspected there was something odd about the situation. Men who find refuge at the back of the trade winds usually have something to hide from.'

'Indeed,' he said dryly. 'A very philosophical attitude.'

Outside the Lodge she held out her hand for her pack and said formally, 'Thank you very much for—for everything. Goodbye.'

But her plans to get rid of him quickly were countered by Tui, who marched out through the door and said, 'Are you coming in for lunch, Slade?'

He shook his head with an appreciative smile. 'No, I have to get back to town.'

'You're missing hot scones,' Tui said, adding slyly, 'With whipped cream and home-made tamarillo jam.'

'You know how to tempt a man; unfortunately I have an appointment in Auckland. Thank you for the offer—can I take you up on it another time?'

'Any time,' Tui told him.

He looked at Alli, green eyes gleaming. 'Take care,' he said, and turned and strode lithely back to the big car.

Left to herself, Alli would have gone inside, but Tui stayed and waved, so she did too, because anything other would have produced questions.

'What we used to call a real dish,' her boss said with pleasure. 'He's got presence, that one. I'll bet the women chase him.'

'He might have made up his mind which one he'll have,' Alli said, thinking of Caroline's eminent worthiness to be Slade Hawkings's wife. He'd said she had no right to object to anything he did, but he was meeting her that night at the Thorpes', whoever they were.

And Caroline Forsythe struck Alli as being quietly determined.

'Ah, well, better get back to work,' Tui said with a last wave that was answered by a short toot as Slade's car took the cattlestop. 'You're looking a bit tired. Have a nap, and then take Lady out for a gallop along the beach.' She waited until Alli hefted her bag before asking, 'When are you going to see him again?'

'Not ever,' Alli said, the words resounding heavily inside her head.

Tui laughed. 'It's not like you to be coy.'

'I'm not!'

Her employer said cheerfully, 'Well, let me tell you something, girl—that man wants you. He'll be back, you'll see.'

Don't do this, Alli said silently. 'I didn't know you were a mind-reader.'

'Can't do minds, but I'm pretty good at body language,' Tui returned smartly. 'He's tracking, Alli. If you don't want him, you'd better start running.'

CHAPTER SEVEN

TUI bustled into the kitchen, her expression a mixture of sly humour and surprise. 'You're a close-mouthed one,' she accused, slapping a newspaper down on the table in front of Alli. 'You haven't said a word about last weekend in town with the handsome hunk. Not even about being hounded by the paparazzi!'

Swallowing the final mouthful of delectable chicken pie, Alli turned a startled face to her. 'What?'

Tui flattened the paper out and pointed triumphantly. 'There you are—and it's easy to see it's you! Not like the other one on the beach.'

Sure enough, someone had taken a photograph of Slade's car as he'd driven out of the car park under his apartment building. Stomach roiling, Alli noticed a smile on her photographed face. She couldn't remember smiling—especially not a satisfied smirk like that, hinting at a long night of well-sated passion.

Beneath the photograph the gossip columnist had written, *Who is the woman leaving Slade Hawkings's apartment early—very early—one morning?*

'Didn't you see the photographer?' Tui asked, her curiosity palpable.

'No.'

'Can't say I blame you—if I were sitting beside Slade Hawkings I wouldn't be looking for paparazzi.' Tui pushed the newspaper closer. 'Go on, take it.

That's the second time you've hit the headlines—
you'd better start a scrapbook.'

'I don't want it,' Alli said defiantly, averting her
eyes from the photograph.

'Well, want it or not, you'd better get ready to go
out, because that's Slade Hawkings's car coming up
the drive right now.'

A bewildering mixture of apprehension and awareness churned through Alli. Leaping to her feet, she
muttered, 'Damn! Oh, damn!' and cast a hunted look
through the window.

'Probably the first time a woman's reacted like that
to his arrival,' Tui said knowledgeably. 'I'll go and
meet him—you change into something that looks a
bit more upmarket. Those jeans fit nicely, but your
sweatshirt isn't ageing gracefully.'

'He won't notice.' Not true, she knew.

Her employer knew it too. 'That one notices everything. Go on. What about your nice mossy green
jersey? It looks great with your skin. And put some
lipstick on.'

Alli cast another harried glance through the window before fleeing. Once in her small bedroom she
shrugged into the jersey, but rebelled at lipstick.

He'd come about the photograph, of course. No
doubt he was angry. Well, so was she. Who the heck
had staked out his apartment so early in the morning?
And why? They wouldn't have done it for plain Alli
Pierce, so they must have been tracking Slade.

Head erect and shoulders painfully squared, she
walked back to the Lodge, flinching when a wood
pigeon swooped across her path at eye level about

two feet in front of her, its white breast gleaming in the sun.

Her pulse raced from flutter to jungle beat when she saw Slade in the office. Her first involuntary thought was that lipstick wouldn't have helped anyway. Darkly dominant, he turned to examine her, his displeasure like an icy cloud.

'Come for a drive,' he said, and forestalled her automatic refusal by saying, 'Tui says she can manage without you for half an hour.'

'Longer than that if it's necessary,' Tui said with a stern glance at Alli. 'See if you can persuade her to take her holidays, will you? She's got about ten days in lieu.'

Tui, not now! Self-preservation goaded Alli into terse speech. 'I don't need holidays, and I'd rather walk along the beach.'

No way was she going to let herself be locked in the car with him for half an hour.

Equally crisply, Slade returned, 'Fine. Show me the way.'

Once outside the Lodge she asked, 'Have you heard how the boy in a coma is?'

'Recovering well,' he said. 'No brain damage, apparently.'

'Thank God,' she breathed.

'He was lucky; if he's got any sense he'll learn from it.' Slade looked around as she indicated the boardwalk between the dunes. 'This is very different from Valanu.'

'Much colder,' she said with a half-smile, then swung into tourist mode. 'Tui and Joe and the local conservation society are doing their best to reclaim the dunes. They've got them fenced off so no one can ride through them, and, as you can see, it's working.'

Out on the beach, the sun smiled down on rows of waves sweeping onto the beach in perfect formation. Lithe black forms played amongst them—surfers. The water was warming, and very soon they'd be able to discard their wetsuits.

'Why are you here?' Alli asked.

'Partly to discuss the photograph in the paper today.'

'We can't do anything about that,' she said with a casual shrug. 'No one knows who I am, so any gossip will die. What I'd like to know is why the photographer was so conveniently there. Do you usually have paparazzi staking you out?'

'Occasionally.'

'Why that day?'

'I doubt if it was anything to do with you,' he said shortly.

She glowered at him. 'Of course it wasn't. You're the celebrity, not me.'

'I'm not a celebrity, and gossip doesn't worry me.'

'I'm afraid I don't have your lofty attitude to it. Finding myself in the newspaper made my skin crawl. What I can't work out is where the photographer was. I didn't see anyone.' Probably because she'd been too busy sending Slade sideways glances through her lashes. The thought of people all over New Zealand drawing conclusions from that smile rankled.

'It was taken with a telephoto lens from the park across the street.' Slade stooped and picked up a length of driftwood, hefting it a moment to test its weight before hurling it into the surf. Watching it sink below the waves, he said, 'Don't worry about it—you won't appear in any other photographs.'

'I'm glad to hear it.' Keeping her eyes on the distant place where the beach receded into a soft salt-haze, Alli frowned against the sun. A painful needle of hope pricked her heart, tormenting her with its persistence. To get rid of it once and for all, she said briskly, 'It's very kind of you to come and tell me this, but really I didn't expect it. A phone call would have been enough, although that wouldn't have been necessary either. After all, we've already said our goodbyes.'

Stone-faced, Slade scrutinised her. 'You surely don't believe that Marian would just hand over a photograph of your mother and send you on your way without another word?'

She'd believed just that—after all, Marian's farewell had seemed more than definite.

'I see you do.' His voice was dry. 'You're her only relative.'

'For which she's probably devoutly thankful.'

'You were certainly a shock to her,' he admitted. 'However, she doesn't want to lose sight of you.'

Alli didn't know what to say to this. In the end she contented herself with a cautious, 'That's very kind of her, but I don't want her to feel any sort of obligation to me.'

'It comes with the territory,' he said shortly. 'Families work like that. She's asked me to tell you that she'd like you to stay with her so you can get to know each other.'

His expression didn't alter, but she knew he disapproved of this latest development. Alli fought a brief, bitter battle with herself. Marian was offering what she'd always wanted—a family. Yet a deep-seated wariness held her back. 'Caroline—'

Slade cut in with abrupt authority. 'Caroline won't be there.'

Meanly relieved, she said slowly, 'How long does Marian want me to stay?'

'A couple of weeks.' He smiled briefly and without humour. 'I suggested that she and you spend time together at the bach.'

Alli knew that northern New Zealanders used that word to refer to a small, unpretentious holiday house by the beach, but she had a pretty fair idea that Slade's bach would be neither modest nor unsophisticated.

'I don't think that's a good idea,' she said quickly, before she could change her mind.

'Why?'

'I can't believe that she'd want to know me. I must bring back some pretty shattering memories.'

'That won't wash,' he returned instantly. 'She had a very happy marriage with my father—happy enough to rob the fiasco of her first marriage of its sting.'

'I suspect she feels sorry for me. Well, I don't need to be rescued—I've made a good life for myself, with friends and a job I enjoy. I'm not a charity case.'

She angled her chin up at him, the feline enticement of her face temporarily overwhelmed by a cold, still pride. The wind snatched up a handful of dry sand and hurled it at them, making her blink and turn away.

Coolly he said, 'I don't recollect either Marian or I insinuating that you were some orphan in the storm.'

She flushed at the memory that phrase brought back, and he said something under his breath before resuming on an impatient note, 'And since Tui says you're overdue for holidays I can't see why this is such a big deal.'

That, she thought wearily, was the problem—for him it wasn't a big deal. For her it was becoming increasingly so. His suggestion came wrapped with such tempting possibilities—a family, and a man she was starting to dream about whenever she loosened the reins on her will-power...

If only Tui had kept her mouth shut!

'Thank you very much,' she told him firmly, 'but it's not necessary. I wanted to meet my mother and find out why she abandoned me. OK, meeting her is impossible now, but I do know what happened. I have no claim on either of you, so it's probably better that we leave it at that.'

He said calmly, 'You prised the cat out of the bag, Alli; it's too late to thrust it back in again. If you turn Marian down she'll keep trying. She doesn't give up easily.' He looked around at the beach and the surf, the wild exuberance of the gulls whirling over the surf like scraps of white paper, and said dispassionately, 'It wouldn't surprise me if she turned up at the Lodge.'

Alli tightened her lips to hide an odd feeling of being driven discreetly but inevitably into a decision she wasn't ready for. 'She'd hate it. It's very casual and laid-back, and most of our clientele are surfers or fishermen or naturalists.'

'She's adaptable.'

Alli turned her face to the sea. While they'd been

talking the wind had dropped away, and the breeze that feathered across her face now was soft with the promise of summer.

Indecision kept her silent. She longed to forge some links, however casual and fragile, with the only relative she had; it was, she thought with a touch of bitterness, ironic that if she let herself be drawn into the family she faced real danger from Slade.

Well, not from Slade—from her reckless feelings for him. Prudence counselled her to refuse; the heady thrill of being close to him weakened her resolve.

And from what Slade had said he didn't plan to be at the bach.

In the end she licked the salt from her lips and surrendered. 'All right, then. I'll go to the bach for ten days if Poppy, Tui's daughter-in-law, can take my place at the Lodge.'

Within half an hour she was staring at the road twisting away in front of them.

'Your employer still doesn't entirely trust me,' Slade observed, uncannily echoing her thoughts. 'She wasn't going to let you go unless I gave her the address and phone number of the bach.'

'I don't think Tui trusts anyone but her family.'

He nodded. 'Probably a good maxim to live by.' He didn't add, *And sometimes you can't even trust them,* but no doubt he was thinking it.

Alli certainly was.

Slade's bach turned out to be the only house on a hillside above a melon-slice of champagne-coloured sand. The building *was* far from modest; backed by the dark luxuriance of coastal forest, the double-storeyed colonial gem stood four-square and proud, surrounded by a columned verandah with balconies above.

'It looks like a doll's house!' Alli exclaimed, leaning forward as they negotiated the steep drive. 'A very large doll's house.'

'It used to be the original homestead for the area.' With the skill of familiarity Slade steered around a hairpin bend shaded by the thick, feathery canopy of kanuka trees.

Just north of Auckland they'd left the main road and driven through fertile valleys where dairy farms, vineyards and orchards mingled in harmony beneath a range of high hills sombre with a thick, tangled cloak of New Zealand bush.

'I don't see any farm,' she said, beating back a giddy mixture of foreboding and anticipation.

'We've been coming through it for the past fifteen minutes—it started at the first cattlestop. When my father decided he wasn't made for country life he put in a manager's house closer to the road and replanted this hillside in native trees.'

The drive swung around the back of the house onto a wide gravel forecourt. Slade stopped the vehicle and turned off the engine. 'Welcome to my home.'

Alli froze. 'I thought you lived in Auckland.'

'I spend about half my time there. Why? Does it make a difference?'

'No,' she denied, because what else could she say? *Nothing would have persuaded me to come if I'd known you intended to be here too.* Not likely.

He saw through her, of course. Steel edging his words, he drawled, 'Don't worry, I'm off to Tahiti tomorrow.'

Her relief must have shown too clearly, because he smiled—not a nice smile. 'You could come with me,' he suggested, in a tone that was a subtle insult.

Alli scrambled out of the car, her nerves twanging. 'No, thanks.'

He climbed out and reached in the boot for her pack, straightening up with a strap over one shoulder. 'Scared, Alli?'

The direct challenge made her seethe. 'I came to see Marian.'

Tall and dark and compelling, he slung her pack onto his shoulder and walked across the forecourt to a door. It opened as he got there, and Marian beamed at him.

Feeling awkward, Alli followed him and was greeted with a more restrained smile. 'Come in,' the older woman said. 'How are you, Alli?'

'Fine, thank you,' Alli replied automatically.

'I'm so glad you could come. Slade, I've put Alli in the middle bedroom.' Chatting lightly about the journey, she led Alli up the stairs to the top storey and into a room decorated in shades of ivory and soft cream.

Acutely aware of Slade following them with the pack, Alli said, 'Oh, this is lovely. So restful.'

'It has a pretty view out over the bay.' Her hostess gestured towards the glass doors that led out onto the balcony, then indicated another door. 'Your bathroom is through there. We'll leave you to refresh yourself, and when you come on down we'll have afternoon tea. Turn left at the bottom of the stairs and follow the voices!'

The room had been decorated with a deft hand—

an old-fashioned iron-framed bed looked as though it had always been there, and long curtains puffed gently in the breeze. Instead of unpacking, Alli went out onto the balcony and discovered with delight that it was a private one.

She took a deep breath, inhaling the delicious spicy scent of kanuka trees and the ever-present tang of salt.

Time enough to admire the view later, she thought, turning reluctantly away. Swiftly she sorted her clothes into the wardrobe, then picked up her sponge bag and walked into the bathroom.

After washing her face and combing her hair, she tracked the other two to a room that opened out onto the same magnificent view of the sea.

'Slade tells me you drink tea,' Marian said cheerfully. She patted the white sofa beside her and said, 'Come and tell me how you like it. So many young things don't drink tea or coffee nowadays, I find. It's almost a relief to find someone who does!'

After ten minutes Alli decided her hostess's exquisite manners were a mask. But then, she thought with a fleeting glance at Slade's angular face, they were all wearing masks. The time she'd agreed to spend in this lovely house stretched before her like a small taste of eternity.

After she'd drunk her tea Marian commanded, 'Slade, why don't you show Alli around? I'm sure she'd like to see the beach.'

With his trademark lithe grace Slade rose from the chair. 'Come along, Alli,' he said, with a smile as burnished and bland as sheet metal. 'Let me introduce you to Kawau Bay.'

He took her out onto a wide deck, overlooking the

beach, and led her down a couple of steps and across a lawn.

'I love pohutukawas,' Alli said, stopping by one huge tree. 'They symbolise Northland's summers, with their crimson and scarlet flowers like millions of tiny tassels, but they don't grow by the Lodge.'

'They like it rocky,' Slade told her as they went down another two steps to the beach, 'but they can't stand the cold west and southerly winds that sweep over the west coast. Give them a cliff overlooking an island-sheltered bay and they're happy.'

'This is charming.' Smiling, she took in the small curve of sand, the smooth waters of the wide inlet and the shapes of islands to the east. Loyally she added, 'But I do love the west coast. It's so wild and free and dangerous.'

'This can be dangerous too,' he said. 'Don't swim on your own. It's not like the lagoon at Valanu, where you might as well be in a bath.'

'That had its dangers too,' she said quietly, thinking of a friend who had been taken by a shark.

'Life's full of danger.' Slade sounded sardonic. 'The Maori say that the west coast is like a man, strong and virile and warlike, whereas the east coast resembles a woman, beautiful and soft. I'm sure they'd be the first to admit that women can be just as dangerous as men in their own way.'

The sand crunched beneath Alli's feet when they reached the tideline. She stopped there and looked around, her expression grave and considering. To one side, under the low headland that separated this bay from the next, a wharf ran out into deep water. Two boats were tied up to it: a large cruiser, with swept-up bow and all the flashy mod cons, and an elegant dowager from the thirties, solid, dignified and restrained.

'I used to jump off the end of the wharf,' Slade told her. He looked down at her. 'I suppose like me you learned to swim before you could walk?'

'Literally,' she agreed. 'The lagoon was an ideal place to learn, of course.'

'Do you miss Valanu?'

She said thoughtfully, 'Yes, but I always knew I'd have to leave one day. Living there was like living in a fairy story.'

'How long was your father ill before he died?'

'I'm surprised you don't know,' she said, the acid in her voice tempered by irony. 'A year.'

'He didn't think to come back to New Zealand for medical care?'

She looked at the pink-gold sand and said desolately, 'He wouldn't go anywhere, not even to the clinic until it was far too late. I think he wanted to die.'

It was the first time she'd admitted it to herself.

To her astonishment Slade's warm hand enclosed hers. Sensation ran up her arm, quick and shocking as electricity, and somehow transmuted into ripples of slow, wondrous sensuality that gave her a tantalising glimpse of what it might be like to be loved by Slade Hawkings...

Except that it wouldn't be love. So, although the comfort he offered was powerfully seductive, she pulled her hand from his. 'I think he really loved Marian all the time.'

'I won't say forget it, because the past casts long

shadows, but mulling it over and wondering what really happened is a waste of time and mental energy,' Slade said in a voice that lacked any emotion. 'Not only are you never going to know, but I'm sure your father would have wanted you to make your own life without dwelling on his mistakes. Let your parents sleep in peace, Alli.'

She was touched by his understanding, and surprised at the slight abrasiveness of his tone in the latter part of it. 'Yes, sir,' she said meekly.

He laughed, a deep sound that twisted her heart. 'Did I sound like a grandfather? I can pontificate with the best of them.'

'I don't think you were pontificating,' she said, trying hard to be objective. 'It's just that—well, my father was difficult to love because he never unbent, but he was always *there*, and he was reliable. And he was a man of honour. He was respected. When he died they buried him with the chiefs.' She looked up and said simply, 'And he made sure I didn't lie, or steal. He had very strong moral principles, so I suppose I want to know how a man like that could betray someone as comprehensively as he did Marian.'

'He may never have had a grand passion before he met your mother, and been totally unable to deal with it. The thing you have to remember is that he didn't betray you,' Slade said austerely.

She nodded, thinking that this was a strangely intimate conversation to be having with him—one she should not have embarked on. It would, she thought warily, be dangerous to reveal too much of herself to Slade.

She stopped beneath a pohutukawa branch overspreading the beach. A large tyre had been tied to it. 'Your swing?' she said brightly.

'I believe my father was the original user, but this is not the original tyre, or even the original chain. We often have visitors here, and their children love swinging as much as I did.'

The thought of him as a child did something odd to her heart. He'd have been a handful—bold and determined and intelligent…

Banishing such subversive thoughts, she said even more brightly, 'This is a wonderful place for children.'

And almost winced at the banality of her words.

'Indeed,' he said gravely. 'But I hope you will enjoy it too. As soon as I'm gone you'll be able to relax.'

'You don't make me nervous!'

The moment she said it she knew she should have kept her lips firmly buttoned. He looked at her with a gleam of something very like amusement in his green eyes, but as she glared at him it died, to be replaced by a piercing intensity. Alli's mouth went dry. She heard some bird calling, the clear notes dropping into a spreading silence.

He said quietly, 'Then why do your eyes go dark on the rare occasions when you look at me—?'

'I look at you quite often!' Too much—but usually when he couldn't see.

'Mostly you concentrate on an ear, or my hair, or the pocket of my shirt,' he said blandly. 'And did you know that tiny pulse in the base of your throat speeds up whenever I come near?'

Mesmerised, she shook her head. 'I—no.'

By then her mouth was so arid she almost croaked the words. He lifted a lean, tanned hand and touched the hollow in her throat, and any further attempt at speaking was doomed.

How could a fingertip do so much damage? It drained her of will-power until all she could do was stare into his narrowed eyes as though they were her one hope of salvation.

He laughed softly, and then his face came nearer. Alli closed her eyes against the fires in his, but by the time he kissed her mute, imploring mouth she could no longer think. Lost in a rush of heat, she swayed, and he pulled her against his strong body.

It was so familiar, as though she'd done this thousands of times, and she relaxed into him and let his kiss wreak devastation on her already shaken defences.

Her skin tightened deliciously. She shivered as his hand slid down her back to find the curve of her hips, but she didn't pull away.

Whenever she'd kissed other men their arousal had always faintly repelled her, but now, with Slade, she relished the evidence of his desire. Response, white-hot and elemental, scorched through her, washing away inhibitions and fear.

He lifted his mouth, but before disappointment struck he pressed a series of kisses along the line of her jaw. Delight leapt from nerve-end to nerve-end in a tornado of sensation, a delight that turned fierce and wild when his mouth found the soft lobe of her ear and he nipped it, using his teeth with exquisite precision.

That tender nip made her acutely, deliciously aware

of the weight of her breasts, of over-sensitive tips against his hard chest. From her breasts, that wildfire sensation homed in on the place deep inside her, a place that ached with desperate hunger.

His hand swept from her hip to cup the side of her breast; while she dived further into the wilder seas of sensation his thumb played with tormenting slowness over the pleading tip.

Alli's groan was torn from her innermost feelings—a sound, she dimly realised far too late, of surrender.

And then his mouth left hers and he said in a voice entirely empty of any emotion, 'Still positive you don't want to come to Tahiti with me, Alli?'

Stunned, she met coldly calculating eyes, green and cold as crystals. Shame flooded her as she understood that he'd been testing her.

She wanted to slap his arrogant face, and then, humiliatingly, she wanted to burst into tears!

CHAPTER EIGHT

PRIDE gave Alli the strength to pull herself together. She stepped back and said, in a voice she prayed was composed enough to fool him, 'I came here at Marian's invitation, so going to Tahiti would be rude.'

Slade smiled cynically. 'More entertaining, though.'

She shrugged. 'What's fun got to do with it?' She hoped she'd managed to prick his pride with her scorn.

If she had he didn't show it. Instead he stood back courteously to let her walk ahead of him up the steps to the lawn. 'You are, of course, entirely correct,' he said evenly. 'Security is always important.'

She stopped. 'What exactly do you mean by that?'

The gold rays in his eyes glinted. 'What do you think I meant by it?'

'Listen to me,' she said fiercely. 'I don't want money from Marian.'

If she'd thought her directness might throw him she had misjudged the man. He said, 'I'm glad to hear that.'

But she could tell he didn't believe her.

Clenching her jaw to hold back a bitter disillusionment, she said, 'I'm not going to try and justify myself—people with prejudices are rarely able to change them even when confronted by the truth. And this *is* the truth. I've managed my life so far without asking for money from anyone; I don't intend to start now. Besides, if you think I'm here to feather my nest why did you bring me?'

'So you didn't *ask* Barry Simcox on Valanu to pay you three times the rate everyone else was paid?' he observed, taking her elbow and turning her towards the house.

Even that brief touch shortened her breath. 'He said that because I was a New Zealander that's what I should be paid...'

Her voice faded under Slade's sardonic glance. How stupid she'd been! Of course she hadn't been entitled to the extra money; Barry had made the decision after her father died, no doubt thinking she needed extra income.

'It seemed logical at the time. I just didn't think,' she said lamely. She dragged air into her lungs and spoke into the disbelieving silence. 'I'll pay back every cent I owe you, and you can stop testing me. It's harassment and it's demeaning.'

He said on note of mockery, 'Indeed? I don't want your money—you've more than repaid it with your excellent ideas about getting Sea Winds back on its feet. As for harassment—while it was happening I could have sworn you enjoyed it just as much as I enjoy kissing you.'

Stunned, she risked a glance at him, and met a coolly watchful scrutiny. Pleasure it might have been, but he'd been in complete control of the situation— unlike her, weakly melting in a puddle at his feet!

He added, 'And making love to you would be pleasure also.'

Colour stained her skin. 'Lovemaking as a test of integrity? The thought makes my flesh crawl.'

'If we made love,' he said silkily, 'I suspect that by the second kiss everything but carnal appetite would fly out of the window.' He watched more colour roil up through her skin, and went on, 'I had reason to distrust you. You must admit that your first letter to Marian was aggressive enough to make her very wary.'

Alli flushed. 'I was—angry, I suppose,' she said reluctantly. 'I wanted to know why she—why my mother had abandoned me.'

She still didn't know that, and now she never would. But it no longer overshadowed her life. Somehow Slade had redirected her energies.

I am not in love with him, she thought, sudden panic kicking her stomach.

Slade said, 'It's the primal fear of children, isn't it—abandonment by the mother? I was barely four when my mother died. I remember the shock and the bewilderment and the terror.'

Heart-wrung for the small, heartbroken boy whose mother had left him in the most final of ways, she said quietly, 'At least I didn't know what I was missing.'

At the bottom of the steps leading onto the deck, he said, 'Just to set the record straight, if it *is* money you're interested in you should know that Marian's income is derived from a trust fund. She can't touch the principal.'

Alli went white. 'I find you utterly disgusting,' she retorted, and ran ahead, across the deck and into the house.

Once in her room she paced the floor until she regained control over her seething emotions. That final cut from Slade had been calculated to wound.

Why did he dislike her so much?

Because their kiss had affected him as much as it had her?

She dismissed the thought immediately. Slade had probably been born with an innate knowledge of how to please a woman, a skill honed by practice.

So kissing her hadn't been a big deal for him. Oh, he'd wanted her—but lust came easily and meant very little.

After all, she wanted him...

She walked out onto the balcony. While she'd been pacing the sun had dipped low in the west, its long rays gilding the bush behind the house and edging the clouds with gold. Slade was strolling towards the beach, tall and confident, his gait as smooth as the silent, killing lope of a predator.

A knock at the door made her jump.

It was Marian, smiling and pleasant. 'I thought you might like to come down and have a drink with us. A fax has just come through for poor Slade—he has to leave tonight instead of tomorrow morning, so we'll have dinner early.'

Alli glanced down at her clothes. 'Should I change?'

'Oh, no—you look lovely.'

Something in Marian's tone made her look up sharply, but the other woman had already turned away. 'See you in a few minutes,' she said brightly, and disappeared down the stairs.

Slowly Alli tidied up before following her hostess.

It was an odd evening, with hidden tensions prowling beneath the relaxed, sophisticated surface. As always, Marian was the epitome of a gracious hostess, and Slade was amiable enough—in the fashion of a well-fed tiger.

Apart from the lazy appreciation in his tone when he spoke to her, Alli thought savagely, you'd never know that he'd kissed her senseless.

At last she could bear it no longer. 'Do you mind if I go up now? I'm a little tired.'

Slade's gaze rested thoughtfully on her face as Marian said, 'Not at all. Do let me know if there's anything you need, won't you?'

'Thank you.' Pinning a smile onto her mouth, she turned to Slade. 'Have a safe journey,' she said quietly.

'Thank you.' His eyes were more golden than green, and unease brushed like a feather across her skin.

Back in her room, she sat down in the darkness and tried to work out what had set her intuition jangling.

Something about this situation didn't ring true. Slade warning her off was logical. She suspected he trusted very few people, and only after they'd earned it. And he was hugely protective of his stepmother.

Frowning, she struggled to make sense of a jumble of hunches and faint impressions.

Marian had asked her to come here, supposedly so that they could get to know each other, but beneath the older woman's superb manners lay something else, something so tenuous it was only visible in swiftly concealed flashes.

Not dislike, she thought carefully, not even caution.

If she had to pin it down to one thing, she'd say that Marian was in the grip of tightly controlled fear.

'No,' she said aloud, shaking her head.

She had to be over-dramatising, because why should Marian be afraid of her? And if she was, or if that emotion she sensed wasn't fear but something else—say, repugnance—why had the older woman asked her to stay?

It simply didn't make sense. 'So you're wrong,' she said slowly.

The hands in her lap suddenly clenched. She didn't know what Slade thought or felt or wanted, but he'd made no secret of the fact that he didn't trust her.

Perhaps he'd seconded his stepmother's invitation in the hope that Alli would reveal herself in her true colours, whatever they were?

That made sense. Marian might not be able to spend more than the interest from her trust fund, but in comparison to most people she was rich. And Slade was well on the way to becoming a billionaire, if he wasn't already. So when a relation showed up out of the blue naturally they'd want to know what sort of person she was.

Especially as her parents seemed to have had very low moral standards!

'In other words,' she murmured to the distant sound of an outboard motor puttering quietly around a nearby headland, 'you're on trial because they think you might be like Alison.'

As a child, when she'd imagined finding her family she'd always assumed they'd accept her freely and lovingly. Maturity had tempered that first innocent belief, of course, but it still hurt to know that any hope of acceptance lay in convincing Slade she hadn't come to prey on Marian.

She woke to a silent house and a breathless dawn shimmering across the bay; the trees on the hillside were cloaked in mist that streamed upwards in transparent tendrils.

It was an exquisite beginning to a time that was an odd mixture of laughter and tension. Marian had a keen sense of humour that often bubbled over into wit. She never asked personal questions, but she wanted to know about Alli's life in Valanu, and Alli was happy to tell her.

But gradually, while they walked along the beach and beneath the canopy of the forest Slade's father had planted, while they ate meals at charming vineyard cafés and explored the lovely countryside around, visiting a marine reserve to watch fish that approached them without fear, Alli realised two things.

One was that whenever someone approached Marian she introduced Alli as a friend, chatted briefly, and then moved on within a few minutes.

The other was that Marian revealed very little of herself. She didn't speak of her family, and she never talked about the sister who had borne her husband's child—she didn't even mention Slade often.

While the sunny days passed in golden serenity, Alli's resolve hardened. Once this was over she'd go back to the Lodge and pick up her own life. She might even, she thought, go to Australia. And although that felt like running away, it also seemed eminently sensible, because she didn't want her presence to upset this woman she was learning to like.

Once she asked, 'Did my father have any relatives?'

Marian looked at her with quick sympathy. 'He was an only child, and his parents died young. He never spoke of cousins or any family.'

'And you?' Alli ventured.

Marian's face closed down. 'A few distant cousins in England—I've long lost touch with them.' Smoothly she moved onto another subject, cutting off any further questions.

Not that Alli would have asked them.

Almost a week after Slade had left, she was walking down the stairs when she heard what sounded like a soft groan from behind her. Every sense alert, she swung around. The housekeeper usually spent the couple of hours after lunch at her cottage in the next bay, so Marian was the only other person in the house.

The silence suddenly turned oppressive, weighing Alli down. It had to be Marian, who always rested for a short time after lunch. But it hadn't been a snore...

Oh, well, she could only make a fool of herself. Biting her lip, she turned and ran lightly up the staircase. Outside the door to Marian's room she stopped and listened, but heard nothing else.

Her swift, tentative knock seemed to echo, but she heard a faint noise from inside the room. She drew in a deep breath and said, 'Marian? Are you all right?'

No answer. By now worried, she said, 'I'm going to open the door.'

Carefully she turned the handle and peeked in. The curtains were drawn, but through the dimness she could see the older woman in an armchair; she seemed to be asleep, but something about her stillness alarmed Alli.

'I'll just check that you're all right,' she said quietly, and approached the chair.

Halfway across the room she realised that Marian's eyes were open and fixed on her. Was she enduring some sort of waking dream?

Tensely, Alli said, 'Are you not well?'

No answer, although the muscles in the older woman's throat moved as if she tried to speak. Panic punched Alli in the stomach; she took Marian's hand and said steadily, trying to fill her voice with reassurance, 'Marian, wake up. It's all right, you're at home and in your bedroom...'

Silently Marian continued to stare at her—no, Alli thought with a shiver, *through* her. Something was seriously wrong. She said, 'I'll ring Mrs Hopkins and get her to call an ambulance and your doctor. Don't worry—you'll be fine.'

She lifted the telephone by the bed and punched the housekeeper's number through, only to get no answer. Mrs Hopkins had been going out to lunch, she suddenly remembered.

For the second time in too few weeks she dialled 111 and, when an impersonal voice answered, explained exactly what had happened.

'Just talk gently to her,' the voice at the other end said, before the connection was cut.

Alli picked up the older woman's flaccid hand and said quietly, 'An ambulance is coming. It won't take long—you'll soon be in hospital, where they can find out what the problem is.'

The housekeeper arrived back from lunch just before the ambulance, and packed her employer's bag while the medics stabilised her. Feeling like an extra leg, Alli hung around, desperately concerned. Gone was Marian's smiling charm; she'd suddenly become old and desperately fragile.

'Should we ring Slade?' Mrs Hopkins worried as the stretcher carried Marian down the stairs. 'It looks like a stroke to me.'

'He's in Tahiti, but I don't have an address.'

'Neither do I.'

They looked at each other, the housekeeper clearly seeking guidance.

Alli said, 'I'm going to the hospital with Marian— I'll drive her car down. Can you ring Slade's office and tell his PA or secretary or whatever he has what's happened, and where Marian is?' She hesitated, then said, 'I'll ring you as soon as I can and tell you what's happening.'

Clearly relieved to have something to do, the housekeeper nodded. 'All right.'

Torn by fear and compassion for the woman in the ambulance ahead, Alli drove Marian's powder-blue Mercedes down, wondering if this attack had been her doing.

And things got worse at the hospital. She didn't know the simplest things about Marian beyond her name; she had no idea what other illnesses she'd had, what the address of her Auckland residence was, or even how old she was.

But at last a very small, pale Marian was in bed,

hooked up to an array of instruments. She still hadn't moved. Her helplessness shocked Alli. For the first time she felt some sort of kinship with the older woman.

'I'll stay with you,' she told her, touching her hand. 'But first I need to ring Mrs Hopkins and reassure her that you're in good hands.'

Marian looked gravely at her, not a flicker of comprehension in the blue eyes. Sick with worry, Alli took herself off to the payphone.

The housekeeper asked urgently, 'How is she?'

'She hasn't changed, and no one's told me anything, but she's comfortable. Have you heard from Slade?'

'Yes, he's on his way home and expects to be here later tonight. He's going straight to the hospital as soon as he gets in.' Mrs Hopkins sighed. 'It must be a stroke. It doesn't seem possible—she's not a day over fifty-five!'

'If it is a stroke, it's not a death sentence,' Alli said crisply, hoping she was right.

'Of course it's not, and they can do such wonderful things now, can't they?' She sounded too emphatic, as though trying to convince herself.

On the way back, Alli discovered she was trying to convince herself too. Refusing to accept any possibility but a full recovery, she sat down by the bed, taking Marian's lax hand in hers. It seemed ridiculous to feel as though her touch helped, but in this world of beeping, gurgling machines it was at least human. Some distance away a baby cried—thin, exhausted wails that made her ache.

She never had any idea how long she sat there,

holding her aunt's hand and talking quietly to her; as night closed down outside she dozed, and was more than half asleep when a subtle scent brought her to full alertness. Twisting in the chair, she looked up at Slade's face, its strong framework sharply prominent. Her heart leapt and she scrambled up awkwardly, so relieved to see him that she almost burst into tears.

He said quietly, 'How is she?'

Marian's eyelids flickered. 'Better now you're here,' Alli said, her voice wavering. 'Look, she knows you've come.'

He leaned over the bed, kissing his stepmother's forehead. 'It's all right,' he said in a deep voice. 'It's all right, Marian, I'm here.'

And, to Alli's astonishment, Marian's mouth moved a little and she sighed.

Slade straightened. 'Alli, there's no need for you to stay now. Sally Hopkins says you've got Marian's car?'

'Yes.'

He tossed her a swipe card. 'It's the key to my apartment. I've ordered a driver to take you back there.'

She caught the card and said, 'But how will you get in?'

'I have a spare.' He looked keenly at her. 'And, Alli—thank you.'

CHAPTER NINE

ALLI woke with heart thudding and ears on full alert. Darkness pressed heavily on her until a subdued noise from the kitchen indicated that someone had just closed the fridge door.

She drew a sharp breath and swung her long legs over the side of the bed, hooked her thin cotton dressing gown over her shoulders and padded warily out into the hall. More homely sounds reassured her—the clink of a glass on the granite bench, the sound of a tap being turned off—but it was a muttered swearword that told her who was there.

Slade couldn't have heard her, but before the door was more than a few centimetres open he'd swivelled around to face her. She froze, because in his face she saw a cold anger that stopped her mind.

Something had gone very wrong.

'It's all right,' she said quickly.

He put his glass of water down on the bench and said politely, 'I'm sorry—I thought I was being quiet.'

'How—how is Marian?' she asked, aching for him.

'She's recovering. It wasn't a stroke.'

So what was wrong? Alli said tentatively, 'That's wonderful—isn't it?'

He drained the glass and set it back on the bench with controlled care. 'Indeed it is.'

The discipline of his expression and tone sent shivers scudding down her spine. 'Do they know what the problem is?'

He shrugged and leaned back against the bench. Hooded eyes dispassionate yet intent, he said, 'So far they don't know, but the general conclusion seems to be that she's exhausted and needs to conserve her strength, so her body just shut down. They expect her to revive when her unconscious decides it's safe to do so.'

She asked quietly, 'Was it me?'

Unreadable eyes searched her face with icy detachment. 'I don't know.'

The words came without conscious thought. 'Why is she afraid of me?'

'She's not afraid of you,' he said with sharp emphasis.

'I'll leave tomorrow.' Her voice was flat and completely determined.

'It's too late for that.'

Her skin tightened. She thought she could feel the tension like an electrical force around them, a dark turbulence shot by lightning.

Desperate to get away, she turned and fumbled for the door handle, her heart blocking her throat when he said something explosive beneath his breath and reached past her to wrench open the door as though he'd like to tear it off its hinges.

Startled by the silent ferocity of his arrival, she flinched.

For several seconds they stood facing each other. Alli's breath came faster as her heart sped up; she saw the colour in his eyes swallowed up by darkness, and knew that her own were widening endlessly...

Afterwards she could never remember who broke first—whether the hand she held out to ward him off found his muscled forearm, or whether his hand lifted to touch her face.

Whatever, when he cupped her cheek and said her name in a low, raw tone excited anticipation prickled through her in a response as elemental as it was dangerous.

Some hidden part of her brain warned that she'd be sorry, but it was swamped by an intense, entirely carnal desire. 'Yes,' she said simply, knowing exactly what she was agreeing to and unable to think of any good reason why she should deny herself this.

For her own protection she wouldn't dare stay in contact with Slade, but before she disappeared from his life she'd know what it was like to make love with him.

Freed at last from fear, she opened her mouth beneath his hard demand to give him what he wanted— what they both wanted. His arms tightened around her, and she gasped when he picked her up and shouldered his way through the door, carried her down the hall and into a bedroom. Once inside, he set her down on her feet, supporting her by the shoulders. His scrutiny was so intense she could feel the gold and green flames licking around her.

'I've wanted this since I first saw you in Valanu,' he said harshly.

Passionate anticipation bubbled up through her. Eyes enormous, she nodded.

As his lips found the spot where her neck joined her shoulders he pushed her dressing gown from her shoulders, his hands sliding on down her back to the hem of her T-shirt. They were warm and strong, and instead of whipping the shirt over her head they slid up beneath it.

Alli shivered, and he said, 'Are you cold?'

'No,' she whispered, on fire from her skin to the aching centre of her being.

This time he kissed her lips, tormenting her with the teasing lightness. A hungry little noise escaped from her throat and she looped her arms around his neck, trying to bring his mouth closer to hers.

One lean hand cupped her breast. Alli shuddered, and dragged an impeded breath into famished lungs. Electricity arced from her breast to the pit of her stomach, relaying the torrid effect of his touch through every cell in her body. Her breasts felt heavy, so responsive to his caresses that she was sure they throbbed.

'You can touch me if you want to,' he murmured, and gently bit the lobe of her ear.

Excitement whipped up higher through her body. Swiftly she unbuttoned his shirt. The heat from his taut skin seared her fingertips, and when she looked up the gold lights in his eyes scorched through the ragged remnants of her self-control.

The soft material of her T-shirt became an unbearable barrier; she fumbled for it, hungering for the feel of his skin against hers.

'What is it?' His voice was a sexy rumble. 'What do you want?'

'I want—I want—' Unable to formulate the words, she pushed the sides of his shirt further apart. Finally, she muttered angrily, 'I want you.'

Black lashes almost shaded the green and gold glitter of his eyes. 'Good, because I want you too,' he said, the words such a blatant act of possession that they stopped the breath in her throat.

She stared at him, meeting his narrowed eyes with a hot shiver of urgency that exploded like a fireburst inside her. 'Then take off your shirt,' she said raggedly, unable to dissemble.

Her whole body longed for him, craved him, demanded him—if she didn't get what she wanted she thought she might die of need.

He dropped his hands, stepping back in silent invitation.

Dry-mouthed, she pushed his shirt from his shoulders and down over the corded muscles of his arms, letting it fall to the floor.

The impact of his bare torso hit her like a shockwave. Lamplight burnished the powerful shoulders and chest to bronze, sheened the sleek skin of his flat abdomen.

Any more, she thought feverishly, and I'm going to swoon at his feet!

Slowly, her heart beating a tattoo in her ears, Alli pressed the flat of her hand over his heart, reassured when she felt its uneven beat driving into her palm. Against his formidable masculinity her hand looked pale and fragile, but at her touch his chest rose sharply.

Acute, gratified pleasure pierced her. She wasn't the only one lost to this overwhelming desire. Although she couldn't make herself look into his face, his silence and his stillness reassured her; with tentative strokes she examined the texture of hair and skin until her questing fingers reached a small dark nub.

Again that sudden rise of his chest startled her, and she whipped back her fingers, only to have them clamped beneath his. He said, 'Surely you know that men and women aren't very different? We like to be pleasured, and your touch pleasures me.'

At last Alli gathered enough courage to look into his face.

What she saw there shocked her; raw need hardened his features and gleamed in his eyes, so concentrated she could feel it blasting into her. A rising tide of passion almost blocked her thoughts.

'Take off your T-shirt,' he said, the words soft and rough.

For a second she hesitated, tempted to demand that he do it, but something about removing her own clothes appealed to her pride. Head held high, she met his eyes as she slid the material over her head, lowering it to stand before him in nothing but narrow cotton briefs.

Silently he reached for her, and some part of herself was comforted because his hand shook slightly when it mimicked hers, his thumb lightly stroking the pink centre of her breast.

Sensation arrowed through her, white-hot and elemental. Slade pulled her into the heat and strength of his body, and she sighed and linked her arms around his neck and mutely offered herself to him.

He kissed the hollow at the base of her throat, and then his mouth slid slower, tasting, teasing, exploring each gentle curve with slow, erotic finesse.

And when he reached one pouting, pleading centre

he drew it inside his mouth. Her knees buckled and she cried his name in a voice that betrayed every molten, reckless sensation bursting through her.

Slade lifted his head and surveyed her with narrowed, glittering eyes. Wonderingly, she touched his mouth, so uncompromising, yet capable of delivering such intense delight. He kissed the tip of her finger, and when she slid it into the moisture inside he bit the skin tenderly, his sharp teeth sending a thrill of desire though her.

'I can think of a better place for us to be,' he said, and he picked her up.

The coolness of the sheet beneath her back and legs provided an intriguing contrast to the urgency that sizzled through her; she relaxed onto the pillows, only noticing then that he had taken her into his bedroom.

When he'd finished undressing she forgot everything in the wonder of watching him with complete absorption, every cell in her body throbbing in desperate anticipation.

On Valanu she'd seen male tourists in bathing suits so minuscule they might as well have been naked. Now she realised that the scrap of material swathed around hips had made a huge difference; without it, Slade was magnificent.

She swallowed, wondering feverishly if this was going to work...and if she should perhaps tell him that she'd never made love before.

He came to the edge of the bed with the silent, powerful grace that marked him out from other men. Alli held herself still while he eased down beside her, and for the first time she felt the shock of nakedness—skin flexing against heated skin, the slow play of muscles, the feeling of being overwhelmed by sheer masculinity.

Utterly exposed, her skin colouring under his gaze, she buried her shy face in his shoulder and nuzzled him, and his faint, tantalising scent filled her nostrils, replacing the nervousness and fear with a quiet, lovely certainty. She kissed his shoulder, and then sank her teeth delicately into the skin before licking it.

Big body shuddering, he said harshly, 'For this once, let me do the work, all right?'

Surely he didn't expect his lovers to lie there and do nothing? Puzzled, she glanced up and met his eyes, almost flinching back at their heat.

He finished, 'Otherwise it might well be over before we start.'

Perhaps it had been a while since he'd made love.

That thought excited and pleased her, as did the suggestion that he wasn't in full control when he was with her.

She touched the taut skin over his solar plexus. 'I can do this, though?'

'Only if I say the times tables aloud while you do,' he said, and kissed the throbbing little hollow in her throat, and then the curve of her breast.

This time when he took the tight little bud into his mouth and began to suckle she thought she knew what was coming, but the exquisite sensation wrested what was left of her control from her and sent it whistling down the wind. Alli groaned, her hips rising instinctively against him.

'Not yet,' he said softly, moving to the other breast

while one hand discovered the small hollow of her navel and the curve of her hip.

Ravished by delight, she made an incoherent little noise in her throat and ran her hands up his back, relishing the way the muscles bunched beneath her palms.

His hand moved further down. She wanted him to continue more than life itself, yet she stiffened in instinctive fear.

'It's all right,' he said softly. 'I just want to see if you're ready.'

Ready? Oh, she thought longingly, she was so ready—couldn't he sense it? But, although she arched upwards again in silent plea, he sat up and reached for something on the bedside table.

She watched as he donned the condom, and wondered at her pang of sadness.

Slade looked at her. 'The first time I saw you I thought of the golden pearls of the Pacific, because your skin glows like them. You seem to radiate light and heat and passion.'

And he kissed her again, and this time when his hand reached the cleft between her legs she relaxed, most of her apprehension vanishing like mist in sunlight, and groaned harshly when he stroked her there before easing a finger inside.

Torn by unbearable anticipation, she didn't know whether to obey the urge to pull him over and into her, or the equally strong one that insisted she lie there and let this voluptuous lethargy carry her wherever it wanted her to go.

Slade took the decision from her. He moved over

her and pressed against the slick entrance. Slowly, carefully, he eased a little way into her.

Her breath locking in her throat, Alli stared up into his face, a savagely carved mask of primal appetite.

'Am I too heavy?' he asked.

'No.' She swallowed and tried again. 'I like it.'

And, indeed, lying like this beneath him was probably the closest to heaven she was ever likely to get.

He frowned, but pushed a little further, focusing entirely on her, his face clamped in severe lines as he controlled the hunger she sensed in him.

And control it he did, tormenting her with his restraint until pleasure burned through her and she whimpered with the need for more than this slow, cautious progress. Driven by wild desire, she gripped his hips, holding him against her. He thrust deeper, and again even deeper, releasing a hunger that smashed through her final barriers.

Alli twisted recklessly against him, clasping him with inner muscles she'd never used before until he gasped, 'No!'

Too late. Slade's mouth came down on hers and somewhere in the fire and passion of that kiss, his control shattered.

Joined with him in ecstatic union, Alli closed her eyes and welcomed each movement of his powerful body, her every sense so acute it was almost painful to feel his heat and the coiled steel of his body as he took her with him into unknown regions of the heart.

No wonder desire brought down kingdoms!

Nothing could be more wonderful—but then a cresting wave of sensation flung her up, up, up into a storm of sensuality, holding her on a knife-edge of intolerable rapture.

Slade, she thought with what was left of her mind. Slade...

Somehow she forced her eyes open, filling her vision with his darkly drawn face, the fire in his half-closed eyes and the gleam of sweat on his body. Her lips formed his name as, overwhelmed by unbearable ecstasy, she cried out and convulsed beneath him.

Slade went with her on that incredible journey into the heart of the storm, eventually collapsing on the distant shores of satiation, his chest heaving as she cradled him in her arms and let ebbing passion lull her into dreamy bliss.

When he moved, her arms tightened around him in the instinctive need to keep him so close that nothing could ever come between them. But he used his great strength against her, rolling so that he lay beneath her.

He lay there for long moments, her slim, lax body light on him, her flushed, languid face half turned on his chest and her eyes already closing, and swore silently and at length.

How the hell had it got to this? You blew it, he told himself grimly. You knew it was dangerous, but you couldn't bloody well control yourself.

When he was seven Marian had come like sunlight into his life. Slowly, suspiciously, he had trusted her enough to let himself love her.

And now, only a few miles from here, she lay in a fugue of exhaustion caused by the girl who slept on him in sensual exhaustion. He tensed as Alli yawned and rubbed her cheek against his chest in a gesture as artless as it was seductive. His body stirred beneath her, and mentally he cursed his total lack of will-power where she was concerned, each cold, biting word reeking of disgusted derision.

Yet he watched her while she slept, storing up every moment, every second, with the eager greed of a miner hoarding gems.

Alli woke to silence. Dazed by unremembered satisfaction, she stretched and yawned, wondering sleepily why her body felt different—and then she remembered and shot upwards, searching the room for a man who wasn't there.

She was alone, and in her own bed. Well, Slade's spare bed, she thought, feverish colour scorching her cheekbones. He must have carried her there after they'd made love and she'd gone to sleep in his arms.

Jumbled images of the previous night circled her brain. She might have been a virgin but she could recognise expertise when she came across it. Making love was no novelty to him.

So, while it had been a slow, incandescent trip to heaven for her, for him it had just been fun as usual.

She listened, but the apartment was silent. Biting her lip, she got out of bed, flushing again when she realised that she was still naked. A neat pile on a chair indicated that Slade had returned her discarded clothes too. Hastily she made for the bathroom.

After a shower she dried herself down and examined her gleaming, naked body for sombre moments in the mirror. Apart from lips that were fuller than usual—and more tender—she looked the same. Several marks, too slight to be called bruises, startled her. His beard, she thought confusedly, must have been just long enough to abrade the delicate skin of her breasts. At the time she hadn't noticed.

'But then you probably wouldn't have noticed a firework display on the end of the bed,' she muttered, and hid her face by towelling her hair dry.

He had left a note outside her door. Stupid dread constricting her heart, she stared at it for a second before stooping to pick it up. Without salutation, his bold writing informed her that he had gone to the hospital, where he would see her when she was ready. He'd signed it with a formal signature, *S T Hawkings*, and added a postscript. Marian had been transferred to a private hospital; he'd sketched a map showing her how to get there.

'I wonder what the T stands for,' she said, folding the paper and putting it in her pocket. 'Thunderbolt, perhaps?'

But although her tone was wry, silly tears stung her eyes, and she found she couldn't manage anything for breakfast beyond a cup of coffee.

That downed, she left the apartment and drove sedately across town, stifling her nervousness at the traffic with the hope that Marian had recovered consciousness.

The new hospital was considerably more upmarket than the public one Marian had been taken to the previous day. She was shown into a kind of ante-chamber to Marian's room, and while the nurse went in to check that the patient could see her Alli absently noted bowls of flowers and a couple of pretty, unassuming landscapes on the walls.

When the door clicked open again she looked up, startled when she met Caroline Forsythe's eyes.

'She's not up to seeing you just now,' Caroline said calmly. 'Slade is with her, so I'll wait with you.' She glanced out of the window. 'In fact, I'd like to go for a walk, and they have lovely gardens here. Would you like to come with me?'

'I think I'll wait here, thanks,' Alli said. The other woman, she saw, wore an engagement ring.

Caroline shrugged. 'It'll be a while.' She surveyed Alli. 'You look as though you've spent a sleepless night too. Come on, some fresh air will do you good.'

'How is she?'

'Conscious,' Caroline said readily, holding open the door to the hallway. 'Which is wonderful. But she says she feels very tired. What on earth happened?'

Caroline's voice had softened when she spoke of her godmother, so Alli got to her feet, feeling mean for refusing to accompany her when the other woman was so clearly worried. Together they went down in the lift, and, while they walked in gardens sweet with the first roses, she told Caroline what had happened.

'It must have been terrifying,' Caroline said sympathetically. 'Oh, look! That glorious Graham Thomas rose is out in the arbour. Let's sit down here for a moment, shall we?'

She waited until they were both seated, then asked, 'What happened to give Marian a heart attack?'

Alli stopped abruptly. 'A heart attack! But Slade said it was something else!'

'Did he?' Unsmiling, Caroline examined her. 'Why did you agree to stay with her when you must have known that the mere sight of you brought back the most hideous memories?'

Her words shocked Alli into rising, but Caroline's

hand shot out swiftly as a snake and fastened around her wrist.

'Listen to me,' she said flatly. 'I don't know whether you've been told what happened with your parents, but if you haven't, it's time you were.'

CHAPTER TEN

DISCONNECTED thoughts tumbled in jerky confusion around Alli's mind. She said, 'I don't think—'

'Normally I wouldn't intrude,' Caroline interrupted with pleasant firmness, 'and I owe you an apology for what I said to you the first time you came to see Marian, but I was awfully worried about that meeting.'

Alli couldn't hide her shock, but Caroline went on smoothly, 'Yes, I know all about it. I did mention that Marian and I were very close, which is why I'm telling you that your presence is so utterly traumatic for her. It's not personal, believe me. Your mother—'

Interrupting in her turn, Alli said shortly, 'I know what my mother did.'

'It must have been a terrible thing to hear.' Caroline glanced at her engagement ring. 'When we were in Tahiti Slade thought that perhaps the best thing to do was get Marian to go to counselling.'

She paused and turned the ring so that it caught the light. Alli's fragile composure fractured into splinters.

Frowning, Caroline looked up. 'Now he's worried she might have a complete nervous breakdown, and he feels responsible because he agreed to let you meet her.'

Nausea roiled in Alli's stomach; so he had taken Caroline to Tahiti—and did that ring mean an engagement?

Caroline explained, 'He is very protective of Marian. But then, strong men usually are protective of their women.'

Fortunately she didn't seem to need an answer, because Alli couldn't think of a word to say.

'She was so good to him as a child. His father was away so much that he'd sent Slade to boarding school when he was only six, but Marian insisted that Slade come home. She was a real mother to him, so you can see why he's so worried about her now.'

Ungracefully Alli stood up. 'I've always seen that. Neither of them need worry about my presence any more.' The words felt thick, clumsy on her tongue.

'I'm so sorry.' Caroline scrambled to her feet. 'It's an impossible situation for you all.'

'So impossible that the simplest and quickest way to resolve it is for me to leave,' Alli said with a twisted smile.

'Yes, that would probably be the best thing. Only— Marian will feel obliged to keep in touch.'

Alli shrugged. 'If she doesn't know where I am she won't be able to,' she said briskly. 'Give her my love, won't you? And tell her I never meant to hurt her.'

'Of course I'll do that.' She asked, 'Do you have money?'

'Enough.' The thought of borrowing money from this woman, however kind she was trying to be, stung.

Caroline nodded. 'Good luck, then.'

Three months later Alli slung her bag onto the Valanu wharf and turned to wave to the Californian couple who'd let her work her passage from Sant'Rosa. 'I'll be back in a couple of days,' she called.

They waved, and she walked into the port.

Heat settled onto her like a steamy blanket, in spite of the soft caress of the trade wind. She looked about, wondering how she could feel so little for the place she'd called home. Now, home was wherever Slade was.

Because she didn't dare think about him, she pushed the memories into the furthest recesses of her mind. Tui at the Lodge had overcome her fear of computers and e-mailed that Marian was fine, and that Slade had come looking for her in a towering rage the day after she'd grabbed her clothes, offered a garbled explanation for her departure, and run.

Her instinct to take refuge in Valanu like a wounded animal, hadn't been the most sensible decision, but then she hadn't been thinking sensibly when she'd left New Zealand.

Staying at the resort was out. Not, she knew, that Slade would come looking for her now; no doubt he and Marian were only too glad to see the back of her. If he was engaged to the lovely, oh-so-helpful Caroline, the last thing he'd want was a one-night stand hanging around!

Grimly she headed for a small, somewhat sleazy motel close to the port. This was only a respite, anyway. During the long, lovely nights when she'd kept her lonely watch on the vast Pacific, she'd worked out a plan of campaign.

First a pilgrimage to her father's grave and a visit to Sisilu.

Then she'd sail with her nice Californians to Australia, find a job there, and make a life for herself without Slade, without Marian, without emotional complications.

Just like her father.

Of course, she thought with wintry resignation, you could call a broken heart an emotional complication. Hers didn't seem to want to heal; so far time hadn't eased the intense ache of loneliness and longing at all. Instead of outrunning her pain, she'd carried it with her.

At the motel the receptionist took an impression of her credit card, showed her a small room overlooking the swimming pool, and with mechanical courtesy wished her a good stay on Valanu. Alli didn't know her, which was a relief.

A weary lethargy imprisoned her in the room for the rest of the afternoon; she lay on the surprisingly comfortable bed and watched the ceiling fan whirr around, only stirring at sundown to shower and change into a pareu. Tomorrow she'd contact Sisilu, but right now she needed air.

The decision made, she was locking the door when a prickle of danger lifted the hairs on the nape of her neck; she froze, then glanced over her shoulder. Slade was striding towards her through the purple dusk like a silent, lethal force of nature. Heart jolting into a pounding, uneven rhythm, she fumbled the key into the lock again. But before she could take refuge inside a hand closed over hers and pulled the key out of her fingers.

'You took your damned time getting here,' Slade said icily.

She was shaking, her vision dim and her mouth dry, the faint, essential scent of him swamping her senses. 'What—is it Marian?' she finally managed to ask huskily, refusing to look any higher than his throat.

'She's fine,' he bit out. 'She is, however, worried sick about you.'

Possessed by fragile joy, she didn't move, couldn't speak.

'Aren't you going to ask what I'm doing here?'

'So tell me,' she said thinly.

His fingers on her elbow brooked no resistance. 'We'll go back to the resort. This place is about as unsavoury as Valanu gets.' He opened the door of a waiting cab and ushered her in.

She should have resisted, but running away hadn't helped; this meeting might provide some sort of closure, free her from the intolerable weight of lost expectations and forlorn hope. They sat for the short trip in silence; Alli knew she should be shoring up her defences, but it was too late for that.

Was this, she'd wondered on those long night watches while she'd gazed at the familiar impersonal stars wheeling in their grand patterns, how Alison had felt about her father—so in love that anything, even betraying a sister, had meant little?

In that case, why had she abandoned him and their child? Why had she told Marian that she'd aborted the baby? Nothing made sense—but then, loving Slade didn't make sense either.

He took her to the private entrance of the honeymoon suite; once inside she stared around, avoiding the part of the room where Slade stood watching her. 'It's been redecorated,' she commented jerkily, trying to impose some sort of normality onto this meeting.

'The whole resort's been refurbished.' He sounded completely fed up. 'Alli, look at me.'

His will forced her to obey. 'Is Marian fully recovered?' she asked.

'Once she got over the shock of your flight,' he said caustically. 'What the hell drove you away? Caroline said you were fine when you two walked in the garden together.'

Presumably Caroline had done her best to save Marian worry. 'I left because my presence stressed Marian so much she couldn't cope. I know she tries to think of me as an ordinary human being, but every time she looks at me she must see my mother.'

'Possibly,' he said bluntly, 'although she certainly doesn't blame you for your mother's behaviour. I thought I'd convinced you of that.'

'She suspects I might be like Alison, amoral and greedy.' When he frowned, she persisted, 'So do you. That's why you assumed I was sleeping with every man who came near me, wasn't it?'

'Is that what you believe?' He came across the room to her, and when she took a step back he stopped. In a voice she didn't recognise he said, 'I have never lifted my hand to a woman, and I will never hurt you, Alli. But I need to know something.'

Her lips formed the word. 'What?'

His hard, beautiful mouth tightened. 'Whether you were a virgin when we made love.'

Astonished, she blinked. 'Why does it matter?'

'It does. I had you targeted as a thoroughly relaxed young woman, taking sex lightly and without angst.'

'Promiscuous, in other words.'

He hesitated, then said, 'No. You grew up here, where sex is considered a recreation.'

'Only,' she said tartly, 'for those who aren't married, or promised in marriage. My father didn't seem to worry about the islanders' attitude to sex, but he certainly didn't approve of liaisons when it came to his daughter.' She smiled bitterly. 'Amusing, isn't it? I just thought he was old-fashioned.'

'He knew—none better, I imagine—what damage it can do,' Slade said. 'You haven't answered me.'

Admitting that she'd been a virgin would be giving too much away; only a woman in love would risk so much for a man who wasn't in love with her. 'I don't think it's any of your business. I haven't asked you how many women you've made love to. Where did you get the idea that I was Barry Simcox's girlfriend?'

He shrugged. 'His attitude, which backed up what I was told—that you had broken up his marriage.'

'Who told you that?'

'It doesn't matter,' he said briefly. 'Is it true?'

'No. His wife hated Valanu, but she wouldn't admit it because she'd pushed him to take the position. I think she'd imagined living some sort of colonial life, sipping gin slings and flirting with the unmarried men while servants did all the work.'

At his snort, she said with a bleak smile, 'She was a romantic, I suppose. The reality—a failing resort with precious little social life of the sort she'd expected—was a huge shock, and she didn't try to hide how miserable she was. So she looked around for something to give her a reason to leave.'

'You don't think finding you naked with her husband was reason enough?' He spoke neutrally, but she saw the flicker of a muscle in the angular line of his jaw.

She said curtly, 'I'll bet whoever told you that didn't say that I was screaming at the top of my lungs at the time.'

'What the hell was he doing?' An intimidating, ice-cold combination of steel and fire, Slade's voice sliced through her words.

'He was rescuing me from a cockroach,' she told him with acid precision. 'I was changing in the staff bathroom for the evening show when it jumped me.' She shuddered. 'Have you ever seen one? They're huge and black, and this one dropped from the ceiling and ran down my back. I freaked. Barry was on his way to the men's room, and when he heard me yelling he thought I was being attacked. He came tearing in and saved me. I was hauling my pareu on when his wife came racing in and called us every foul word under the sun. She left on the next plane with their little boy.'

'He wanted you,' Slade said harshly. 'Everyone knew it.'

'Possibly, but I didn't want him.' She stared at him with flat defiance. 'Why is this important—or even interesting—to you? I might be my mother's daughter, but I don't sleep with married men. Or engaged ones.'

He said abruptly, 'Are you insinuating that I'm engaged?'

Her conversation with the other woman suddenly took a new twist. Caroline hadn't said she and Slade were engaged, though she'd certainly implied it. Had she set Alli up?

'Are you?'

'No.' His mouth closed like a clamp. 'I have never been engaged. And you still haven't answered my question.'

He might not be engaged, but that didn't mean he was interested in Alli as anything more than a convenient outlet for his sexual needs.

Pain burning like fire through her, she walked across to the window and looked into the garden, barely noticing the lush greenery starred with flamboyant hibiscuses and the pure, sculpted blooms of frangipani.

'Yes, I was a virgin,' she said quietly, uneasily aware of anticipation running through her like an underground river.

'I thought as much,' he said remotely. 'I'll take you back to the motel and you can pack; we're leaving in half an hour.'

Anticipation died a swift, brutal death. She reached out and clutched a curtain. 'Why?'

'I don't seduce virgins,' he said savagely.

'So if I hadn't been a virgin you'd leave me here?'

He stared at her as though she'd suddenly gone mad. 'Don't be an idiot.'

Outraged, she snapped, 'And you didn't seduce me—I wanted to make love to you! So don't go thinking that because you had your wicked way with me you owe me something! You don't. As an introduction to making love it was pretty damned good, but women nowadays don't feel any obligation to marry the first man they sleep with.'

She could have bitten her tongue out once she realised what that final sentence indicated. Sickly she waited for a put-down.

He said levelly, 'Marian asked me to bring you back.'

Bewildered, Alli shook her head. 'Why? My presence brought about her collapse—'

'It didn't.' He spoke with such assurance she turned to search his hard face for some indication of what was going on. Without any success. The mask was back in place, hard and unreadable and totally ruthless. He finished, 'She has something to tell you.'

'More secrets?' she asked wearily, shoulders slumping. 'I've had enough of them. In fact, I've had enough of this whole situation.'

'Tough. You don't have the choice. You've tried running away, but wherever you go I'll be one step behind until you've heard what Marian has to say. After that no one will follow you if you want to go. But she's not going to rest until she's told you what she has to say. And I'm not going to leave you until you've heard it.'

Alli dithered, but in the end she said with grim resignation, 'All right, then. I'll come back—but after that I'm going.'

At Auckland airport, the luxurious private jet was met by a car that dropped them off at Marian's apartment.

Outside her aunt's door Alli took a deep, jagged breath, astounded when Slade's hand covered hers, its warmth and strength offering support.

She didn't dare look at him, and before the door

opened he let her go, but she carried his touch inside her like a fire in the depths of winter.

Marian stood there, the anxiety in her blue eyes fading to relief. 'My dear,' she said, putting out a hand to draw Alli inside. 'Oh, my dear, I've been so *worried* about you!'

'I've been worrying about you too,' Alli said on a half-laugh, 'but you look great!'

'Such a silly thing to have happened! Exhaustion, the doctor said, and the aftermath of the flu, and I seem to have developed a propensity for fainting now and then—as you know only too well, poor girl. But it won't happen again; I've promised Slade and my doctor that I'll eat regularly and sleep eight hours a night, and take iron pills every day! Come through and tell me what you've been doing.'

Slade allowed them ten minutes of catching up before saying, 'Marian, you're procrastinating. Tell Alli what you told me.'

Marian sighed. 'You were such a dear little boy—what happened to turn you into a despot? Very well, then.' She sipped water from a glass, but instead of returning it to the table beside her she clutched the tumbler. In a level, almost conversational tone she said, 'First of all, Alli, your mother and I were half-sisters.'

'Half-sisters?'

'Yes. We had different mothers. I think my father loved Alison's mother, but he was a snob, and she wasn't the sort of person who satisfied his rigid ideas of suitability, so after Alison was born he married my mother, who came from a good family.'

She looked past them both, seeing other faces,

other events. Stunned, Alli said, 'He abandoned his first family?'

Marian looked tired. 'Oh, no.'

But she didn't continue straight away. Instead she took another sip of water, replaced the tumbler on the table and gazed down at the large diamonds winking in her engagement ring and gold wedding ring as though seeking strength from them.

Alli almost screamed with the tension, starting slightly when Marian began again in a tightly controlled tone.

'He kept them in a nice house in the nearest city. We lived in the country. I knew nothing about it, of course, and neither did my mother. My first intimation of the situation came when I was seventeen and had newly left school. Alison tracked me down and told me everything.'

She stopped again, her expression blank. Swallowing to ease a dry throat, Alli thought desperately, *Please, finish it quickly!*

'Keep going.' Slade's voice was calm and steady.

Marian took a deep breath. 'She wanted to tell me that she resented being supplanted by me. Even more, she resented the fact that she was a bastard. She called herself my father's dirty little secret, and it was obvious that she despised both her parents—but especially her mother. She told me that everything I had, everything I'd been given—a good school, social standing, legitimacy—had been stolen from her.'

She hesitated before adding, 'She told me she wanted it back.'

When Alli shivered the older woman nodded sadly. 'She meant it. I didn't know what to say to her—to be truthful she frightened me—but after that she stalked me. I didn't realise that's what it was, of course—in those days we had no word for such a thing. But wherever I went, there she was too. Sometimes it would be several weeks before I'd see her, but she always came back. She sent me birthday cards and Christmas cards.'

'Why didn't you tell your father?' Alli asked, horrified.

'I couldn't bring myself to.' Marian seemed to have retreated into herself. 'My mother might have found out, and I knew how dreadful that would be for her. Marrying Hugo was such a relief. I loved him very much, and he lived on the opposite side of the world. But Alison was in the crowd outside the church when we were married.'

She swallowed and sipped more water.

Slade frowned, hard gaze fixed onto his stepmother's beautiful face. 'Go on,' he said gently.

'So we came to New Zealand, and it was as though a weight fell off my shoulders. For a year I was happy. When I discovered I was pregnant Hugo and I were so delighted and life was wonderful—and then she knocked on my door.'

Alli sat frozen, her hands clasped so tightly in her lap that her knuckles shone white.

'To cut a long story short,' Marian said tiredly, 'she was obviously pregnant.'

Any remaining colour drained from Alli's skin, taking all warmth, all joy with it. It was like standing on the brink of a precipice, unable to stop herself from taking the fatal next step.

Marian said, 'She boasted that she'd seduced Hugo

and that the baby was his. Her next step, she said, was to stake a claim to my inheritance. My mother had died shortly after my wedding, and Alison was certain she could persuade our father to change his will so that she was the only beneficiary of the trust fund he'd planned to set up for us both. It was the first I'd heard of that, and it meant, of course, that he acknowledged her legally as his daughter.'

With the blood drumming in her ears, Alli heard Marian say, 'Of course I asked Hugo if it was true. He was desperately ashamed, but he admitted it. She had sought him out and dazzled him—he said that he loved me, but he hadn't known what passion was like until he met her.'

Alli swallowed.

Remorselessly Marian's soft voice went on, 'I sent him away, and then I lost my baby—it was born premature and died within minutes. Then I had a telephone call from Alison—as soon as she'd heard that my child was dead she'd aborted hers. She said—she said—' She shuddered.

'I don't want to hear anything more.' Alli's voice grated on the words.

Marian looked at her with eyes filled with tears. 'I know. But—it's almost over.' She waited until Alli gave an almost imperceptible nod. 'She said I could have Hugo back if I was desperate, but that whenever we made love he'd be holding her in his arms.'

Alli said numbly, 'I'm so sorry.'

Slade's hands closed over her shoulders, holding her in place, his strength pouring through them into her body.

Tonelessly Marian finished, 'Some months later I

was contacted because Alison had been killed in Thailand. Apparently she was on her way back to England and our father when she stepped into the path of a truck. I never heard from Hugo again; when we divorced it was all done through our solicitors.' She closed her eyes.

'She must have been mad,' Alli breathed.

Marian opened her eyes and said simply, 'She was seriously disturbed. But I married Slade's father and we were very happy together. I don't think even my half-sister could have stolen him from me.'

'I wish I'd never contacted you,' Alli said fiercely. 'I had no idea of the pain I'd cause.'

'My dear, it's better to know the truth,' the older woman said. 'Although when I realised who you were I was afraid.'

'That I'd be like my mother?' Alli produced a twisted parody of a smile. 'I don't blame you.'

'You're not like your mother,' Slade said calmly. 'You are a warm, responsible, loyal woman.'

His words warmed some part of her that had been frozen since the first time she'd met Marian, in this very room, and heard her talk about her sister's betrayal.

'Exactly,' Marian agreed. 'I couldn't have said it better myself.' She looked at Alli and seemed to be readying herself to say something, but Slade cut in.

'That's enough for the present. Both of you are exhausted, and anything more can wait until later. Come on, Alli, I'll take you home.'

For the first time since they'd met at the door Marian smiled. 'What a good idea.'

Alli said, 'We can't leave you alone.'

'Don't worry about me. I feel as though I've just shed a huge load from my shoulders. I'm sorry you had to hear that, but knowledge truly is power.'

Alli got to her feet. 'I think he—my father—realised that he had always loved you,' she said slowly. 'He cut out the newspaper article about your marriage to Slade's father and kept it with his marriage certificate. That's how I discovered who you were and where you lived.'

The older woman looked bleak. 'Between us, Alison and I made a wasteland of his life.'

Slade said with ruthless logic, 'You had nothing to do with it—it was his decision to be unfaithful. And he spent years working hard and extremely well for the people of Valanu. I don't think his life was wasted.'

On the way home Alli said, 'Thank you for what you said about my father.'

'It's the truth,' he said negligently. 'You can be proud of him because he did an enormous amount of good in the islands. Possibly he tried to atone for his mistakes that way.'

'I hope so,' she said quietly. She didn't want to think about her mother. Fixing her eyes on the harbour, smiling beneath a late summer sun, she asked, 'Where are we going?'

He'd told Marian he was taking her home, but she had no home now.

'I think we've had this conversation before,' Slade said coolly. 'I'm taking you back to the homestead.'

She sneaked a glance at him; he turned his head and smiled at her, and she knew that she would go with him wherever he asked her to.

If he wanted her she would expect nothing from him but fidelity. As long as she had that, she thought dreamily, she'd be happy.

They drove silently through the blue and gold evening, arriving at the bay with a glory of scarlet and crimson and apricot streaked across the western sky.

'It's going to be a fine day tomorrow,' Slade remarked, lifting her bag from the car.

Alli stood a moment, inhaling. 'I missed the scent of the kanuka trees,' she said, smiling at him without reserve.

'I always do too.'

He put her in the room she'd occupied before. When she'd showered and changed into a pareu, a restrained length of cotton the colour of the red highlights in her hair, she came shyly down the stairs to join Slade on the deck as the first stars trembled into life in the indigo sky.

He handed her a glass of champagne. 'Here's to the future.'

'I'll definitely drink to that.' But she'd barely tasted the delicious wine before she set the glass down, saying, 'You knew about my mother, didn't you?'

'Yes. When the researchers I employed finally tracked down the details of your birth I told Marian. She was shattered, and it all came spilling out.'

Keeping her eyes on a pair of fantails fluttering around just beyond arm's reach, their black eyes bright as small beaks snapped up night-flying insects, she asked, 'Is that why you distrusted me so much?'

Accurately divining her secret fear, he said bluntly, 'You were right when you accused me of testing you. I did wonder if you were like her, damaged in some basic way. I bought the resort so that I could use it as a lever if I had to.'

'You paid a lot of money for a lever that might not have worked if I'd been like my mother,' she said quietly.

He shrugged. 'It had good prospects. The area was already settling down, and I had plans for it. I didn't expect to lose anything on it. Then I got there and realised that Barry couldn't look at you without salivating.'

'No!' she said indignantly.

His brows rose. 'Trust me. I know,' he said dryly. 'And, although I was as suspicious of you as hell, I hated that.' Irony and something like self-derision curled his mouth. 'Of course I wouldn't allow myself to realise it, but I was jealous—black, deep, dog-in-the-manger jealous. So I offered you the chance of staying on Valanu and saving your friends' jobs.'

Alli said, 'I should hate you.'

His eyes gleamed. 'But you don't, do you?'

She bit her lip.

The fantails' high-pitched squeaks faded as they flew into a bush. Slade put his glass down and walked across the deck to join her in the gathering dusk.

'You stayed on Valanu. Even when you left, you made no effort to contact Marian. And when you thought that your presence was causing Marian real problems you left. As far as I can work out Alison would have pulled the world down around her in flames to get her way. She didn't care a bit about hurting other people.'

'No.' It hurt so much to say that single word.

Very deliberately he said, 'You are entirely normal.' And he turned her into the circle of his arms. When she stared at him, her face coloured by the dying glow of the sun, he asked, 'You've had a hell of a shock. Do you want to stay in your own bedroom tonight?'

'No,' she said on a sigh.

If this was all she could have she'd take it. And as he pulled her into his arms she lifted her face to his kiss and felt happiness flood through her, fierce and elemental.

CHAPTER ELEVEN

ALLI lay in sleepy bliss, so replete with pleasure that when Slade came into the room she could barely summon the energy to smile at him.

'Poor you,' she said dreamily. 'Work…and with boring old politicians too.'

He finished knotting his tie and bent to kiss her. Lazily, gracefully, she looped her arms around his neck and matched his kiss with enthusiasm.

'Stop that, baggage.' Slade pulled her hands away and tucked them under the sheet. 'This is a very important meeting, and politicians hate it if you're late. It makes them feel less powerful.'

She loved the way the gold glints in his eyes lit up whenever he looked at her. In fact, she loved everything about him.

'And I'll bet they're not all boring and old and male.' She sat up against the tumbled pillows while he shrugged into the jacket of his superb suit. 'I noticed a couple of very glamorous creatures in the caucus.'

'Not today,' he said.

A tiny arrow pierced her happiness and lodged in her heart. Looking like that, in clothes superbly tailored to fit his wide shoulders and lean hips, Slade was no longer of her world. They had spent the last three days in isolation, cooking for themselves, seeing no one, hearing no one, making love…

In his arms she had learnt so much about herself—
so much about him. Sometimes he gentled her
sweetly into an ecstasy that brought her to tears. Other
times they loved like tigers, fiercely, without inhibi-
tion, losing themselves in rapture so intense she had
to muffle her cries in the hard strength of his shoulder.

In bed, she thought, watching him check the con-
tents of a slim leather briefcase, they were equals.

But outside it? She suspected that while she had
given him her heart completely, for him this fierce
flashfire of desire was enough.

Slade came across and dropped a swift, stinging
kiss on her mouth. 'Go back to sleep,' he commanded, surveying her flushed face. 'You're looking
very slumbrous around the eyes.'

'That isn't tiredness.'

He laughed beneath his breath. 'I'll be back late
this afternoon.'

When he'd gone Alli turned over in the huge bed,
holding back stupid tears. This, she thought wearily,
was what love did to you—stripped you of indepen-
dence and common sense.

The low snarl of an engine brought her upright. She
snatched a T-shirt and a pair of shorts and hauled
them on, just making it to the balcony in time to wave
at the helicopter.

Not that she could pick out Slade. He'd be sitting
up at the front with the pilot—possibly even piloting
it himself. It was stupid to let such a simple thing
make her feel desolated, but as she showered she felt
as though she'd never see him again.

'Besotted,' she informed her reflection severely.
'You're utterly besotted! You should be working out

what you'll do next—at the very least considering some job!—but, no, all you can think of is that you're not going to spend the day in bed with him!'

She pattered downstairs and emptied the dishwasher, then sat out on the deck with a cup of coffee and the newspaper and tried to concentrate on the job market.

Nothing attracted her. Gloomily she put the paper down and watched a tui plunder nectar from the spidery pink blooms of a shrub. The bird's white throat-knot bobbled as it drained the sweetness, and the sun glimmered in blue and green iridescence on its black plumage.

The trouble was she didn't know what Slade wanted from her. She didn't even know what he felt for her. He hadn't told her he loved her—well, she hadn't admitted her love for him either! But he seemed perfectly content to make love to her without any promises or commitment.

This sensuous idyll couldn't last much longer. She certainly wasn't going to let him keep her, even if he wanted to. And she doubted very much whether she'd fit into the life of an extremely rich man anyway; the prospect of spending days like this waiting for him to come home and make love to her did not appeal.

'Certainly not the waiting about part,' she muttered.

What Slade seemed to want from her was mistress duty—no intimacy beyond wild sex and heady passion.

Exactly what her grandfather had wanted from the woman he didn't marry. Did she love Slade enough to stay faithful to him if he married another woman and had children with her?

Never, she thought, pushing the newspaper away with revulsion. She loved jealously and possessively. If he even suggested such a thing she'd—well, she wouldn't submit to such an unequal relationship.

Women nowadays had more options; she had more pride. She'd rather live alone for the rest of her life than be the other woman in a triangle.

Utterly depressed, she watched the tui for a few more minutes, then rang its namesake at the Lodge and asked how things were going there.

'Very well,' Tui said cheerfully. 'Poppy's loving the job, and with Sim going off to school once the holidays are over she'll be able to give me longer hours. What are you doing?'

'Lazing about in the sun,' Alli said brightly.

The tui chose that moment to burst into song. She held the receiver out to the bird, and waited until the clear paean of bell notes had faded to say, 'Your namesake said hi.'

'And lovely it was to hear it,' Tui said. 'Hang on a minute, will you? Something's come up.'

Muffled voices indicated she was holding her hand over the receiver; when she came back on she said, 'I have to go. Great to hear from you, Alli. Come up and see us some time soon.'

You can never go back. Her father used to say that, and, God knew, he'd had enough reason to believe it. There was nothing in Valanu for her now, and nothing at the Lodge either. Her whole life was bound up in one man—whereas she suspected that the big bed upstairs marked the limits of his interest in her.

Certainly there had been no trips to local cafés or vineyards. Did he have friends? Presumably. But he hadn't introduced her to any.

Perhaps he was ashamed of her?

The thought stung so much she spent the rest of the morning scouring bathrooms, changing the sheets on the bed and cleaning the kitchen. She cut a bunch of roses that someone had coaxed into growing behind the house and put them beside the bed, lingering a moment to touch the soft, cool coppery-apricot petals.

After a snack lunch she went down to the beach and sat in the old tyre, missing Slade with an intensity that scared her.

She had no idea how long she'd sat there swinging quietly, when the noise from an engine whipped her head around. Slade, she knew, was coming back by helicopter, so who was this driving down the road in a blue car?

Marian.

Heart lifting, she jumped down and jogged back to the house. Over the past few days she'd spoken to her aunt a couple of times on the phone, and she felt that they were cautiously approaching some sort of understanding of each other.

But it wasn't Marian who stepped out of the car. And Caroline's smile—smug as any cat's, yet oddly set—jolted Alli into wariness.

'Hello,' she said, despising herself for the uncertain note in her voice.

Caroline's smile tightened as she surveyed her. 'Hello, Alli. You're looking well. Can I beg a glass of water from you?'

'Of course!' She led the way into the house, trying to emulate Marian's unforced charm—and failing. Something was wrong. 'Is Marian all right?'

'She's fine.' Caroline's tone was clipped.

The cold patch beneath Alli's ribs expanded. 'Let's go out onto the deck,' she suggested.

Caroline followed her and sat down in one of the chairs. She sipped the water, that faint smile still on her lips, and when Alli's fund of small-talk had dried up she put the glass down with decision.

'You're going to hate me for this,' she said rapidly, 'but I think you should know. Has Slade said anything to you about a trust fund?'

Alli's eyes narrowed. 'No,' she said, before remembering that he'd mentioned Marian's fund when warning her off.

Before she could qualify her answer Caroline said, 'No, I didn't think he had.' She looked around the deck, then back at Alli. 'Your English grandfather left everything in trust to his two daughters,' she said. 'And their descendants. It was quite a substantial amount, although not a fortune.' Her mouth widened into a smile. 'Running two households must have eaten up his capital.'

'How do you know this?'

'Marian told me,' she said, sounding surprised. 'After your mother's death no one knew you existed, so Marian became the sole beneficiary. By then she knew she wasn't going to have any children; after she miscarried things went so wrong she was told there would be no more pregnancies. When Marian married Slade's father she backed his expansion plans with money from the trust fund.'

'What has this to do with anything?' Alli said, worried by the implacable note in the other woman's voice.

Caroline gave an impatient shake of her head. 'I'm sure you know that Bryn Hawkings was a business genius—and Slade is even better than his father was. Hawkings Tourism is now a huge, extremely profitable concern.'

'Why are you telling me this?'

Her companion leaned forward and fixed her with an intent look. 'When you wrote to Marian claiming to be her daughter she knew there was no way you could be that. So she did what she always does—she told Slade and he organised a search for information about you. You know what the result of that was— you are Alison's daughter.'

A chill scudded down Alli's spine. 'Caroline, I know all this. What—?'

'As Alison's daughter, her interest in the trust fund devolves to you.' Caroline sat back, an enigmatic little smile playing around her perfectly painted mouth. 'Any court would grant it to you once you proved who you are—and if the information Slade found convinced him it would convince a court. But even if it didn't Marian is determined to give shares to you. You now effectively own part of his business.'

Alli stared at her. 'Nonsense.'

'It happens to be the truth,' Caroline said calmly. 'You've got power, and if you wanted to you could cause Slade a lot of grief. Being Slade, of course, he's realised this, so he was set himself to neutralise any threat to his business.'

The cold stone beneath Alli's ribs expanded to

press on her heart. 'Tell me exactly what you came to say.'

'I told you you'd hate me.' When Caroline looked at her, Alli saw dislike in her eyes. 'And, yes, I do have an interest in this—I love Slade, and for a while I thought he loved me.' A trace of chagrin marred her smooth voice. 'I'll get over it. But he's going to marry you so that he can control your inheritance, and, quite frankly, I think that's appalling.'

She got to her feet and looked down at Alli, her face devoid of every emotion. 'Beneath his sophisticated surface there's complete ruthlessness. His business is his life. As soon as he realised that you were Alison's daughter he dumped me.' Her glance flicked like a whip across Alli's white face. 'I can see you're in love with him. I pity you. But you should at least know what you're getting into and what sort of man you're in love with.'

And she walked away. Alli got to her feet, but she didn't follow; instead she watched in numb silence as the car sped up the hill into the shadowy darkness beneath the kanuka trees.

Walking like an old woman, she turned and went back to the tyre swing.

She was still sitting in it, keeping the motion going with an occasional kick of her bare foot in the sand, when the helicopter flew over the house and landed— and she was still there when Slade came striding down to the beach.

During those long, bitter hours she'd worked out exactly what she was going to say. But although she watched him until he stopped a few steps away, her aching heart blocked her throat and she couldn't speak.

He said her name, then said it again, this time urgently as he cancelled the gap between them. 'What's the matter?' he demanded, pulling her out of the swing and into his arms.

Steeling her will against the shaming desire to forget everything she'd been told and let herself be seduced into going along with his scheme, she said distantly, 'Caroline called in today.'

'So?' But he let her go, and she felt the concentrated impact of his gaze on her face.

Concisely, without letting her eyes stray above the open neck of his shirt, she told him what Caroline had said.

When she'd finished she heard the small hush of the wavelets on the sand for long seconds before he said, slowly and deliberately, 'She's clever. She's also an eavesdropper, because Marian would never have discussed this with her.'

'That's not an answer,' Alli said tonelessly, hope dying.

'Would you believe any answer I gave you?'

Oh, she wanted to—she craved reassurance like a thirsty man in the desert craved water—but she knew she wouldn't be getting it.

His expression hardened. 'No, you wouldn't,' he said levelly. 'As I said, she's clever. Before you damn me entirely, however, you should know that she sold that photograph of us driving out of the car park to the newspaper.'

'Why?'

'For spite.'

'Because you dumped her?' she said, white-faced.

'Is that what she told you?'

She nodded.

'I've underestimated her,' he said, his tone so evenly judicial it sounded like a death sentence.

'Is it the truth? Were you lovers?' The moment she asked the question Alli knew she'd betrayed herself.

'No,' he said calmly. 'I'm not a sadist, and making love to a woman suffering unrequited love for me would be cruel.'

Alli digested this, knowing she couldn't afford to let the tiny flare of hope grow to anything more. 'How do you know that she took the photo?'

'I have contacts in the press, people who owe me favours. She did it.' His voice was grim.

'Did she lie at all?'

'Not in the facts,' he said with brutal, intimidating honesty. 'It's her reading of my motivation that's way off. And that, I'm certain, was done with malice.'

Alli desperately wanted him to convince her, but she didn't dare trust her own emotions. During that interminable afternoon while she waited for him she'd made up her mind; she couldn't allow hope to weaken her.

A white line emphasising the ruthless cut of his lips, Slade said harshly, 'You'll need to apply through the courts for those shares, but morally, and ultimately legally, you do own them. Marian is determined to give them to you. You could certainly use that to damage me financially.'

'Why didn't you tell me?' she asked, at last voicing the question he had to answer—an answer she dreaded.

He had never looked more arrogant, never more ruthless. 'I didn't intend to make love to you the night of Marian's collapse. I couldn't help myself. And I didn't mean to bring you here—but I couldn't stop myself then, either. In fact, Caroline was right; I brought you here to make you fall in love with me.'

Slade saw the colour abruptly leave her skin, then roll back in a silken wave, but her lion-coloured eyes met his steadily. 'So that you could control me?'

'When have I ever been able to control you? I made love to you because I was completely incapable of resisting you.'

'I don't believe that.' Alli fought for control, because if she gave him what he wanted she'd be asking for a lifetime of regret.

A muscle flicked in his angular jaw. 'Then believe this,' he snarled. 'Why should I seduce you into marriage? That's a lifetime sentence. And if you divorced me I'd have to pay you out more than the worth of those shares.'

'No,' she said angrily.

'Oh, yes—New Zealand's law is fairly tough. Assets are split down the middle. The sensible way to deal with the situation would have been to tell you about the shares, offer you their worth—' with savage precision he named a sum of money that drove the last remnants of colour from her face '—and buy them from you. That way I'd have had control of them without having to pretend that I want you enough to enter into some fake marriage.'

'Then why didn't you do that?' she cried furiously. 'Not that I want them. I'll sign them over to you for a cent, or whatever it takes to make a deal. As far as I'm concerned the money's tainted.'

Holding herself together with fierce will-power, Alli began to walk up to the house. 'Say goodbye to Marian for me,' she said, each word an exercise in determination.

From behind, he said uncompromisingly, 'Just like that? Goodbye and thanks for the memories?'

'What do you expect me to do?' Fists clenched at her sides, she turned on him, allowing anger to give her the strength to say what must be said. 'Let this whole farce go on?'

Hooded green eyes burning in his dark face, he said stonily, 'It's no farce. These past few days have been—magical.'

She made a swift, dismissive gesture. 'Oh, yes, a magical time. You're a superb lover, but it was going to end anyway. We can't stay in bed all our lives. And once it was over—when real life intruded—what then? A practical marriage to safeguard those miserable shares?'

'Practical?' He astonished her with a furious, humourless smile. 'Do you have any idea what you've done to me? Right from the first? Whenever I look at you I can't even think. My brain seizes up so all I can do is want you. Practical? If you leave me I'll spend the rest of my life looking for you, loving you, aching for you—and you call that *practical*? Damn it, Alli, I love you.' He flung out his arm in a gesture. 'Do what you like with the shares. Sell them on the share market if you want to, put them in trust for our children, scatter them to the winds—I don't bloody care! Just tell me you'll marry me.'

Incredulously she scanned his face, its tanned skin stretched starkly over the bold bone structure. He had to know he could make her say anything if he only touched her—yet he stood scrupulously apart, although every muscle in his big, lean body was taut with the effort.

'Oh, Slade,' she whispered. 'Why didn't you tell me you loved me?'

'Why didn't *you* tell me?'

'You must have known,' she muttered. 'For heaven's sake—I was a virgin. Of course I fell fathoms deep in love with you—'

He said with raw intensity, 'Sex isn't love, Alli. I've discovered that these past days. I thought I could bind you to me with sex, make you so addicted to it that you'd never know the difference between that and love. But while I flew home today I accepted something that's been gnawing at my conscience ever since I realised that I love you. I have no right to keep secrets from you, not even the secret of my love. I have to give you your freedom if you want it.'

Her half-laugh, half-sob silenced him. He groaned and reached for her, and then he kissed her and muttered, 'Don't cry. Please don't cry. Of course I love you, my darling, my precious girl. I am utterly besotted with you. Women are supposed to be much better at this sort of thing than men—how could you not know it?'

'I didn't dare even think it,' she wept, clutching him. 'I love you so much, and it hurt so much... My mother... I look like her...and—'

He kissed the stumbling words away. 'I love the way you look. I dream about the way you look. I don't want to hear anything more about your mother. You're you, not her.'

'But Marian—'

He kissed the frown between her brows, and then her eyelids, and then the corners of her mouth. 'Darling, leave those sad old ghosts where they belong, in the past. The future belongs to us and to our children. Do you trust me?'

She nodded. 'This afternoon I didn't think I could ever trust anyone again, but love is trust,' she said. 'Lots of other things too, but trust is the basis for it, isn't it?'

It was a statement, not a question.

'Yes,' he said simply, and this time their kiss sealed their commitment to a future free of the bitter shadow of the past.

EXTRA

HIRED: FOR THE
BOSS'S PLEASURE

She's gone from personal assistant
to mistress—but now he's demanding
she become the boss's bride!

Read all our fabulous stories this month:

MISTRESS: HIRED FOR THE
BILLIONAIRE'S PLEASURE
by INDIA GREY

THE BILLIONAIRE BOSS'S
INNOCENT BRIDE
by LINDSAY ARMSTRONG

HER RUTHLESS ITALIAN BOSS
by CHRISTINA HOLLIS

MEDITERRANEAN BOSS,
CONVENIENT MISTRESS
by KATHRYN ROSS

HPE0209

HARLEQUIN *Presents*

HARLEQUIN *Presents*

kept for his
Pleasure

She's his mistress on demand!

Wherever seduction takes place, these fabulously
wealthy, charismatic, sexy men know how to
keep a woman coming back for more!

She's his mistress on demand—but when he
wants her body *and soul* he will be demanding
a whole lot more! Dare we say it…even marriage!

CONFESSIONS OF A MILLIONAIRE'S MISTRESS
by **Robyn Grady**

Don't miss any books in
this exciting new miniseries
from Harlequin Presents!

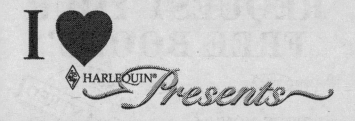

REQUEST YOUR FREE BOOKS!

2 FREE NOVELS
PLUS 2
FREE GIFTS!

PASSION GUARANTEED SEDUCTION

YES! Please send me 2 FREE Harlequin Presents® novels and my 2 FREE gifts (gifts are worth about $10). After receiving them, if I don't wish to receive any more books, I can return the shipping statement marked "cancel". If I don't cancel, I will receive 6 brand-new novels every month and be billed just $4.05 per book in the U.S. or $4.74 per book in Canada, plus 25¢ shipping and handling per book and applicable taxes, if any*. That's a savings of close to 15% off the cover price! I understand that accepting the 2 free books and gifts places me under no obligation to buy anything. I can always return a shipment and cancel at any time. Even if I never buy another book, the two free books and gifts are mine to keep forever.

106 HDN ERRW 306 HDN ERRL

Name	(PLEASE PRINT)	
Address		Apt. #
City	State/Prov.	Zip/Postal Code

Signature (if under 18, a parent or guardian must sign)

Mail to the **Harlequin Reader Service:**
IN U.S.A.: P.O. Box 1867, Buffalo, NY 14240-1867
IN CANADA: P.O. Box 609, Fort Erie, Ontario L2A 5X3

Not valid to current subscribers of Harlequin Presents books.

Want to try two free books from another line?
Call 1-800-873-8635 or visit www.morefreebooks.com.

* Terms and prices subject to change without notice. N.Y. residents add applicable sales tax. Canadian residents will be charged applicable provincial taxes and GST. Offer not valid in Quebec. This offer is limited to one order per household. All orders subject to approval. Credit or debit balances in a customer's account(s) may be offset by any other outstanding balance owed by or to the customer. Please allow 4 to 6 weeks for delivery. Offer available while quantities last.

Your Privacy: Harlequin Books is committed to protecting your privacy. Our Privacy Policy is available online at www.eHarlequin.com or upon request from the Reader Service. From time to time we make our lists of customers available to reputable third parties who may have a product or service of interest to you. If you would prefer we not share your name and address, please check here. ☐

HP08R

You're invited to join our Tell Harlequin Reader Panel!

By joining our new reader panel you will:

- Receive Harlequin® books—they are FREE and yours to keep with no obligation to purchase anything!
- Participate in fun online surveys
- Exchange opinions and ideas with women just like you
- Have a say in our new book ideas and help us publish the best in women's fiction

In addition, you will have a chance to win great prizes and receive special gifts!
See Web site for details. Some conditions apply.
Space is limited.

To join, visit us at
www.TellHarlequin.com.